BIG CITY SECRETS

Our Shadows Will Remain
Book One

ALEC CHARLES

Big City Secrets
Alec Charles

**Dedicated to Poppy
And for Lula, Willemina and Rumo.**

This edition Copyright © 2016 by Oxford eBooks Ltd.

www.oxford-ebooks.com
Story Copyright © 2015 by Alec Charles

The right of the author to be identified as the author of this work
has been asserted in accordance with the
Copyright, Designs and Patents Act 1988.

All characters and events in this book are fictitious.
Any resemblance to any person living or dead is purely coincidental.

All rights reserved.
No part of this publication may be reproduced, stored in a retrieval system, or
transmitted, in any form or by any means, electronic, mechanical, photocopying,
recording or otherwise, without the prior permission of the copyright owners.

ISBN 978-1-910779-18-7 (Paperback)
ISBN 978-1-910779-15-6 (ePUB)
ASIN B0191YZW4O (Kindle)

Oxford eBooks

In this series:

Big City Secrets
Days of Surrender
Every Open Eye

PROLOGUE

MY OLDER BROTHER wakes me by forcing a clammy hand down over my mouth to guarantee my silence. It's either really late or really early, it's impossible to tell because our bedroom seems like it has been hidden far away from any light and the numbers on my bedside alarm clock don't glow in the dark even though they're supposed to. I can hear Uncle Nick snoring from the next room - his bedroom- as he sleeps off his drink in time for work. My brother asks in a whisper, "Are you awake?"

I nod once for *Yes.*

My brother asks in the same whisper, "Can you hear me?"

I think it's a dumb question to ask seeing how I answered the first question, but I nod again for him anyway.

My brother sighs. "Shit," he says and he removes his hand from my mouth. I can just about make out his silhouette now, kneeling beside my bed. He leans back against the bedside dresser positioned between our beds and runs a hand through his hair. He's sixteen right now and I'm ten. We don't have any grandparents and Uncle Nick isn't really worth mentioning. We figure we're all we really have since dad died and mom ran out.

"Shit," he says again and I open my mouth to talk but he must hear the intake of breath I took because he quickly says, "don't talk, you'll wake Nick."

I wonder what reason I've given him in my ten short years to reach the conclusion I'm incapable of whispering, but I stay quiet anyway and wait for him to start up again.

"I've got to go," he explains. "I can't stay here, not any more. You know how bad he can be! Fucker probably won't even notice I've gone for a week anyway... I don't want you to think I'm *happy* about this," he says, "that I can walk away and leave you here like it's no big deal, because it isn't anything like that at all... Not by a long shot.

"But you'll be okay here," he says, "you really will. You were always his favourite... You were always the son he wanted."

The headlights start crawling up the window before I hear the sound of the rubber wheels creeping along the gravel outside the house. I want to ask who's coming for him - is it a girl he's been seeing or is it one of his friends, but I stay quiet. I stay quiet because I'm real scared Uncle Nick's snoring will stop one second and he'll come rushing into our room the next.

"If I thought you wouldn't be okay," he says, "I'd take you with me," and all of a sudden he's standing tall beside my bed and I see him pick something up - his rucksack - and swing it over his shoulder as he heads for the window, still speaking real softly. "But you'll be fine," he says as he pulls the curtain to one side and outside, the world is the deepest colour of blue you can imagine and the glare of the headlights sting my eyes and make my brother nothing more than a standing, living shadow because that's how close the car is to the house and I'm wondering how long it'll be before Uncle Nick bursts into our room because the lights have gone and woken him up.

"Don't you worry about me," he says as he opens the window as quiet as he can (which is *very* quiet), "and don't ever cry about me. We're both going to be better off because of this," he says and then he's outside and the curtain falls back into place so all I can see is his shadow moving away until it has gone and I hear a car door softly open and close and then the lights move away alongside the sound of those big old wheels creeping back across the stones outside our home.

I wake. It's impossible to tell whether it's really late or really early because it's that dark. For a moment I just wonder why I've woken up like this but then I notice the figure sitting at the end of my bed. It's amazing- it really is - because it's almost exactly six years since the night my brother went and left and now it seems that here he is, sitting at the end of my bed. I'm thinking he must have come back for me; that he figures I'm old enough to pull my weight and live with him now or he's finally saved enough money to buy property someplace and he wants me to take the spare room and live a life of luxury. But then I notice the smell of cigarettes and beer and whisky and I fall back down to earth with a bump on realising how it's only my Uncle Nick. He knocks back the contents of the bottle and rubs the back of his wrist across his mouth and I stay as silent and as still as possible, hoping he'll figure I'm asleep and leave or he'll realise he's stumbled into the wrong room and make his exit.

"You boys," he finally says, "are really something. You know that?"

I don't answer. I don't make a fucking sound. Does he know I'm awake or is he just thinking aloud? I don't have the slightest idea and I sure as hell don't want to find out.

"Yeah," he says with a nod, "you know. That's one thing I can't say about you - you're not stupid. But you're *something*," he says. "You get that from your mother," he adds before knocking back more alcohol.

"Bunch of ungrateful cunts," he says with a shake of his head. "I tell you how Phil saw your brother not so long ago?" he asks and it's a real struggle for me not to sit up and bombard him with numerous questions but I somehow manage to remain motionless.

"Yeah," he says, "Phil was on vacation and he figured he'd go drive out to visit his eldest at college while he's on the road. But anyway," he continues, "he stops at some diner in the city and your no-good brother is sitting there - large as life - reading a newspaper and drinking a cup of coffee like it's an everyday occurrence! Phil goes over to him and starts making conversation, and he says your brother looks at him like he's never seen him before in his life. Phil mentions you and me and how he used to come over during the holidays, and your brother is just shaking his head and telling Phil how he's mistaken. Can you believe that? I know I can.

"But Phil... He's trying to figure out if this is some joke he's pulling or something. Phil's saying how he remembers your brother when he was just a kid, and he's saying how he watched him play baseball but your brother just keeps shaking his head and he says Phil has him mistaken for somebody else. Your no-good brother gives Phil a name - a completely different name

- and says that's who he is before he walks out of the diner and climbs aboard the first bus that comes along."

Uncle Nick asks, "Can you believe that? Can you? Walking out on us is one thing... Go on and run away because I don't wrap you in cotton wool and tell you your shit smells like freshly baked cookies. But to change your name? That's a whore's trick," he says. "You get that from your mother."

1

I'M LATE FOR school every day. I just can't get out of bed in the morning, so I stroll in around midmorning and sneak out early whenever I get the chance. Today it's so cold during the walk home that sleet is falling but it magically disappears the moment it touches something. I'm thinking about what my uncle had said, about Phil seeing my older brother in a diner someplace, and I'm wondering if it could be true or if it's just more of his drunken bullshit. I mean, does Nick still work over at the mill or did they get rid of him a long time ago because of his drinking? Fucked if I know. Fucked if I know how they managed to put up with his aggressive nature for so long but tossed him out on his ass once his drinking got too much for them to take. His drinking or his preaching... Believe me - it'd have to be one of the two.

But anyway, I'm just walking along in a world of my own, trying to decide if I should pay Phil a social call while a part of me is also wondering whether my uncle still works at the mill or whether he's doing odd-jobs around town in-between his preaching when the stranger calls for my attention. I hadn't even noticed how close I was to the gas station, hadn't even noticed the stranger standing beside his car, just off the courtyard. The car is one of those long Volkswagens with the wood-panel sides and the trunk is wide open. The stranger is wearing a woolly hat and he has long brown hair and a beard with wisps of pure silver in it. His eyeglasses look a little old and are holding a few beads of water where sleet has landed and although he's obviously wearing more than one layer of clothing, he's shivering in the cold and holding his hands under his armpits.

For a second I wonder if he really did call out to me or whether I imagined it because he's that quiet but then he says, "Yeah, boy!" He says, "How'd you like to buy something neat, huh? How'd you like to help me out of a fix?"

Wondering if this is some guy desperate to offload the grass he was supposed to smuggle someplace else before nerves got the better of him I say, "What're you selling?" taking the first couple of steps closer to his car.

"Whatever takes your interest," he says as he leads me to the open trunk. "You make me a good offer," he says, "and I'll accept it."

A whole bunch of worthless-looking items are spread out on a blanket that must have been in his family for generations and try as I might, I just can't detect the smell of grass or spot any bottles of prescription pills with an interesting name. "I don't know," I say, already sure I'm not going to buy anything but I don't want to shoot the poor guy down so quickly in this weather.

"Come on," he says, moving his hands over the assortment of items as he tries to make a sale before the opportunity has gone. "Look at these," he smiles, moving his fingers against something I've never seen before in my life and so have no idea what use they could possibly have, "or these!"

He's still knocking shit on top of shit when I spot the book with a pyramid on the cover. What looks like a collection of placemats tied together are right next to the book and I notice how the top 'placemat' has a real interesting picture on it so I ask, "What're those?"

"These," the man answers as his face lights up, "are tarot cards. They come with the book," he says, lifting the book with the pyramid on the cover and the tarot cards I had mistaken to be placemats for me to see. "*The Book of Thoth*," the man says, "with the Frieda Harris deck. You do know who wrote *The Book of Thoth*, don't you?"

"No."

The man goes on smiling, refusing to offer any new information before he's sure the suspense is too much for either one of us to take. "Aleister Crowley," he finally reveals. "You do know who Aleister Crowley is, don't you?"

"No."

"No?" he asks as if in horror. "What're they teaching you kids in school, anyway?" he laughs. I feel like reminding him that *this* is Sinclair - a non-existent little town miles from anywhere, and so the teachers only target is to have us able to read well enough or multiply well enough to get a job nearby with no real career prospects - but I don't for fear of the seller telling me how I remind him of his younger self. So instead of telling him *any* of that I straighten my posture and say, "I'm not at school and haven't been for some years, sir. I just have the misfortune of suffering from a rare medical condition that keeps me looking young on the outside while my insides age at an alarming rate."

"Damn," he says despite the fact it's obvious he didn't believe a word of it, "I'm sorry to hear that. But here," he adds, taking a step closer and making it obvious for me to see just how desperate he is on doing so, "let me see if I can grab your attention with these here items you spotted. Crowley," he says, "was in to some really weird stuff; magic rituals and incantations, all sorts of nasty sex..."

I buy the book and accompanying deck for a total of $10. The man laughs and insists I'm robbing him but accepts all I have on me is $10 and not a penny more. "I'll be here for a couple of hours," he yells after me, "I got plenty more stuff if you're interested... Tell your friends about me!"

2

The dining table was built to sit four people. There are two chairs at one side of the table, two on the other. I always sit at my side and Uncle Nick sits at *his* side. Despite how we never usually sit together, we each have our own chair and so four are nothing more than a waste of space.

We never *usually* sit together...

Nick is sitting in *his* chair and I'm sat in mine, the table standing between us. He's wearing his black shirt - the one he wears when he's out preaching as Father Lee - and *The Book of Thoth* is on the table, as are the accompanying tarot cards. He picks up the book and flicks through it for the millionth time. This time he starts at the last page and works his way back to the front cover. His eyes are bloodshot and the smell of beer and cigarette smoke is all over him like ants on an ice cream cone that has been dropped on a hot day, so I figure he'd struggle to focus on the words even if he wasn't having them rush by so fast. He tut-tuts, shakes his head and places the book back down before examining the cards of the deck one last time. Every once in a while, he looks up at me and shakes his head before returning his attention to the deck. Once he's done, he stands up real fast and I think he's going to take a swing at me but I don't flinch - I don't move at all - but my heart takes to beating real fast. Standing with his back to me, Uncle Nick sighs and starts rummaging around inside the drawer beneath the kitchen sink.

"I never saw this day coming," he says, looking out at the night sky while his hand continues searching for something inside the drawer beneath the kitchen sink. "Thought I'd raised you right," he says, "thought I disciplined you when you needed disciplining and I supported you when you needed supporting."

He stops talking; offering me the floor the way a good lawyer gives a condemned man that final chance to tie his own noose.

I don't take the offer. I don't challenge a word he has said. I don't slam my hand down hard on the table and tell him to *stop making so much fucking noise* as he goes on rummaging inside the open drawer. I don't even yawn, which is what I'd like to do more than anything. It's funny what the body can have us do in times of trouble, isn't it? Christ only knows how the old man would react if I went and yawned right now.

"Your brother," he says right as his hand stops moving around, "I could have maybe expected him to have something like that, but not you. Never you," he says as he turns back to the table. He's holding the one knife I don't think I've ever had to use when it came to cooking. The blade must be no longer than an inch, so it's not like it would come in handy for chopping or peeling the vegetables.

"Your mother," he says - shaking his head as he drops back into his chair, "I always hoped she would be the one and only Catholic living under this roof to be led astray, but I was wrong. I just don't understand it. Why," he asks, "would you bring such filth under my roof? What would possess you to bring such material into a house of God?"

He looks at me so long that I have to accept the fact he's waiting for a response. I try to talk - I've no idea what I'm about to say - but something has lodged itself to the back of my throat and I've been completely unaware of it until now so I croak, "Well," before setting to work clearing my throat. I take my time, hoping I'll think of something to say, and he just goes on staring at me.

I picture all the British and European porn films he orders from his specialist catalogue and keeps hidden at the top of his wardrobe. A part of me even wonders if we've jacked-off to the same scenes.

"Well," he says, "aren't you going to answer me? Aren't you going to try and have me understand why you would want to betray me like this?"

He doesn't give me the chance to answer. He leaps to his feet and reaches across the table, taking a tight hold of my left wrist and pulling my arm towards him with such force, I'm not exaggerating saying he could have dislocated my fucking shoulder as the table bites deep into my stomach. I don't offer him any resistance. I can feel every inch of my body trembling but it's more out of the adrenaline rushing around my body than fear. And my vicious uncle just carries on standing there.

I have to admit he has decent composure for a drunk. He doesn't sway from side to side and his hand-eye coordination still looks to be pretty spot-on. He just stands there in silence for a while, looking at something, so I look down to follow his gaze and realise he's looking at the palm of my left hand.

"The Bible doesn't just warn us about other religions," he says, "it warns us how demons can fool us into believing they're helpful spirits... You should know all of this! You should know all of this and you *still* show an interest for this heresy? What if I hadn't found this book?" He asks me, "What then? Would I be coming home to find chicken entrails all over the table? Pentagrams smeared all over the walls in cow blood?

"This," he says, "is for your own good. This is for your own mortal soul. This is so you remember following anything other than the path God has decided for you... to try and second-guess Him... will bring you nothing but pain. Nothing."

He brings the small blade he's holding down so the point is pressing right against my lifeline and he drags it along, always staying right on top of the lifeline. You have to applaud his steady hand as he does it. You have to give him credit for how easily he follows the line on my palm that curves towards the wrist, even when blood is rushing from the fresh cut and making it harder for him to see what he's doing. And I don't flinch or gasp or try to pull my hand back because I don't want to give him the satisfaction. Sure it hurts. You ever strike a match and let it burn out before picking it straight back up again right after? It feels like he's pulling the hottest end of *that* match along my skin. It hurts but it's easy enough to deal with.

3

Eleanor Gayle opens her bedroom window for me and asks me not to be *so loud* as I stumble onto the floor but she soon notices the bloody cloth I've loosely wrapped around my left hand and says, "Jesus! What the fuck happened?" as she places her hands beneath my armpits to try and help me to my feet. I don't need her help but I act like I do, like it's a struggle for me to get up - only to collapse onto her bed.

"Jesus," I smirk. "That's funny."

Eleanor drags the chair from under her bedside table over to the side of the bed and pulls my bad hand towards her. I offer no resistance. I remain flat on my back with my eyes closed and I feel her gently removing the cloth to get a look at my wound. Maybe you're thinking I've only gone over to my girlfriend's place to try and get a little action - to use my still -bleeding hand to get a little sympathy - but you're wrong. Eleanor's old man is the town vet and he's long been preparing his only child to take over his business when he retires. I don't doubt for one moment that she has got surgical skills to rival the best doctor over at the local hospital.

Cold air touches sore, sticky skin. "Jesus," she says for the second time. "What the fuck happened?"

"My uncle's out to save my mortal soul," I reply, eyes still closed.

"Jesus," she says, "your uncle did this?" She's quiet for a second or two. "Fuck," she says, "you're going to need some stitches."

I open my eyes and look to her. She raises her eyes from the wound to look into mine as I ask, "Is it going to scar?"

"Yes," she says, "I'm sorry."

"It's not your fault," I shrug, "and I guess I've always wanted a scar."

She looks back to the wound for a second. "I'll go and get the medical box," she says. "I'll have the bleeding stopped in no time at all."

I smile and reach over to stroke her cheek with my right hand. "You're a doll."

"I'll just be a minute," she says, planting a tender kiss on my right hand. "I'll sneak the supplies past dad," she says, "and I'll bring a little alcohol up and an aspirin or two."

My first serious girlfriend, named after a Beatles song, walks out of the bedroom and closes the door behind her. I hold my hand up in the air and take another look at it. It's bleeding, but not as badly as it was earlier. I'm guessing it only started bleeding again because Eleanor removed the bandage I had made and if she doesn't sew it up soon, it'll keep on opening up and bleeding all over again at the slightest of knocks. A few drops of blood drip free from my skin and land on her bedspread. Her bedroom floor - polished wood without a single rug or patch of carpet - for all I know it already holds a drop or two from when I first entered.

Eleanor cleans the wound using a cotton-ball that has already absorbed a little alcohol and asks, "Are you okay?" as the pain causes me to grimace.

"I'm great," I tell her, resisting the urge to drink a little of the brown liquid inside the glass she has given me. Neat brandy - room temperature with no ice.

"Okay," she says, bringing her eyes down to the torn lifeline, "I'll get this done as quickly as I can..."

Having stitches feels exactly how you would imagine it to; you feel the thread being dragged through one section of skin and then right through another to pull two separate pieces back to one. The palm of my hand - a sensitive area of the human body already - stings like crazy. I look at something on the other side of the room to keep my eyes from her handiwork but I still feel what she's doing. It feels like it's taking forever.

"All done," she finally says and I hear her sever the loose thread with a pair of surgical scissors. I look to my hand and examine what she has done. The skin looks a little puffy and dirty but at least it isn't bleeding now.

"You've done a good job," I tell her.

"Thanks," she blushes, dropping her surgical equipment back into the transparent lunchbox that houses it.

"How long will it be before you have to take the stitches out?" I ask, holding my hand up to her like I'm an Indian chief or something.

Eleanor gently bites down on her lower lip for a moment. "I'm not so sure," she admits, "I'm used to sewing up neighbourhood pets that don't really need stitches to begin with." She pecks me once on the lips and then she's back on her feet with the lunchbox in her hands. "We'll just keep an eye on it and I'll take them out when you're ready," she says. "Now I'll just sneak this back downstairs, bring a little bandaging up to wrap around your hand..."

I smile at her and say, "I'll be waiting."

<h1 style="text-align:center">4</h1>

ELEANOR AND I go through the motions of what I see as our *awkward* lovemaking. I say it's awkward because although God has never blessed me with very much in my life, he more than made up for it 'down below'. So much so that even, that applying a generous amount of baby lotion or something similar to Eleanor's vagina does little to help us. Well, little to help me. I can never push my boner all the way inside her. Even attempting to do that causes her to gasp with pain and I have to start taking it easy because of this. I never get to lose control in the heat of the moment because I'm never presented with a heat of the moment. I always feel like I'm being forced to *make love* when I'm desperate to fuck. Eleanor will always bleed a little because of my giant dick and my joke of 'tearing her a-new-one' never impresses.

Satisfied, she turns off her bedside lamp and cuddles up to me. I wonder how much of her blood is on the sheets right now but she asks all dreamy-like, "You're not going to leave too soon, are you?"

"No," I tell her, "I'll just make sure I'm out of the window before your dad comes in to wake you for school."

"Good," she says, and she gently kisses the side of my hand and strokes my wrist.

"You know something," I say, "sometimes I just can't figure out *why* I'm scared of my fucking uncle."

"Because he's an authoritative figure," Eleanor says, "and your legal guardian."

"Sure," I shrug. "But, you know, even mom could take a punch from him without dropping to the floor like a sack of shit. She must have weighed about as much as three apples when she was soaking wet and still he couldn't put her down easily enough."

Eleanor says, "That's terrible."

"Uh-huh. And the rumours about what he did," I say, "they

have to be just that."

We fall silent. Eleanor eventually asks, "Do you remember her?"

"Who?" I reply.

"Your mother."

"A little," I say with a shrug of my shoulders.

"Do you ever think about the things she liked or what made her smile?"

"No."

"What about your brother?"

"Him," I say, "he just went and forgot all about me. That's all there is to know on that count."

"You don't know that."

"Yes I do. The last thing he ever asked me to do was not to worry about him," I smirk. "He's creeping out of town in the dead of night to start his new life and he tells *me* not to worry about *him*? Jesus…"

"Do you miss him? Ever wonder what you're going to say if you see him again?"

"All I want as far as he's concerned is an apology. I want him to apologise for leaving me high and dry and I want him to admit he did wrong."

I'm dressed and fastening my sneakers, sitting at the side of the bed as Eleanor sleeps soundly. I turn to look at her, so pale and fragile looking in the moonlight, and carefully place a hand over her lips. "Eleanor," I whisper, "are you awake?

"I know you won't understand," I say, removing my hand, "but this is the best thing I can do right now - it really is. But I'll be back for you - I promise. Don't you worry about a thing, you hear?"

The luminous numbers of the digital alarm clock next to her bed tell me it isn't even ten o'clock yet. Opening her bedroom window for the final time, I figure I've plenty of time left to set my things in order.

5

Mrs Delano opens the door and looks at me like I'm something nasty she really won't enjoy scraping from the bottom of her shoe. She's got her hair up in rollers and is wearing a facial mask and a bathrobe that must be twice as old as I am. "What is it," she sighs, "you want?"

"I'm sorry to disturb you like this," I say, "but I was just wondering if I could maybe talk with Mr Delano for a while?"

She eyes me suspiciously and says, "You want to speak with Phil?"

"Yes."

"Well you can," she says, "but you're going to have to go out to the trailer park over on Donovan Drive because he don't live here anymore. Hasn't lived here for at least two summers."

I say just so she'll have to confirm it, "Donovan Drive?"

"Yes," she nods. "You know where it is?"

"Yes," I nod. "Thank you, and sorry for disturbing you," I add, turning to make tracks.

"Wait!" She calls after me, "Why do you want to speak with my no-good husband?"

"I just want to talk with him about something my uncle told me."

"Yeah?" She asks, "Who's your uncle?"

"Mr Lee," I say, "from the mill."

Mrs Delano's eyes open real wide for a second on hearing that, "He's back at the mill?" She says, "Come to think of it - now I see the resemblance. You're *the Father's* kin," she smirks, "no doubt about it. And you want to talk with my Phil, right?"

"That's right."

"Donovan Drive," she says on folding her arms across her chest. "You won't be able to miss him - his is the one with a unicorn painted across the side."

"Thanks," I say, turning to make my exit once and for all.

"You ever need a woman's advice, or even just a spell of company," Mrs Delano says in parting, "you come right back over here. Day or night," she says, "I'll be available."

6

Donovan Drive is a stretch of road that gently curves until it disappears from sight unless you're walking it. You follow that curve and you experience firsthand how the asphalt simply turns to sand and dust, as does the sidewalk. There are a few trees but they always look to be stuck someplace between life and death. Even more trees were chopped down to make way for the trailer park and rundown motel to the back of it. I've heard the motel was there first and it was popular with men wanting to cheat on their wives or vice versa but it's been relatively quiet ever since the trailer park appeared because people don't want to risk being seen going there. The motel owner probably has a deal with the guy running the trailer park - something like trailer park residents are allowed to use the motel bathrooms or something.

I walk by a number of trailers - some look like they could be long deserted while others are just beyond dirty - and eventually the noticeable smell of a barbecue fades into the background and all I'm left smelling is hopelessness. And then I find Phil Delano's trailer near the back. It has to be his, right? What're the odds that two trailers here really do have a large unicorn painted along the side? But it's not as fruity as you're imagining; this unicorn is obviously one you ride into battle in the world of Dungeons and Dragons or something like that.

Standing right at Phil Delano's front door, I wonder how I should go about this. I'm still thinking how I should go about this when the door suddenly opens inwards and Phil, standing with a garbage bag in his hand, almost jumps right out of his skin because he clearly doesn't get too many visitors.

"Jesus!" he yells. It's such a comical sight I have to really fight against the overwhelming desire to laugh. "Jesus," he says a little quieter.

"Mr Delano?" I say it like it is a question even though I'm

certain it's him standing in front of me. A little older, a little smaller, a little fatter, but I recognise him as the man who used to drop by the house when I was a boy.

"Who's asking?" he wants to know.

"I'm sorry," I say, "I'm Mr Lee's nephew. Mr Lee... from the mill?" I ask only to remind him.

"Oh," he says, cheering up on realising I'm no debt collector or something like that - somebody you never want to open the door to. "Sure," he nods, "I remember you," he adds, curving his arm outside - just enough to drop his bag of garbage right to the side of the door. If there's an area in the trailer park for dumping your waste, I gather he intends to go there a little later. "What can I do you for?"

"I'd just like to talk with you for a while."

"Oh," he says, like he has plenty of people needing to talk with him or he's been starved of attention up until this point. "Sure," he smiles as he takes a step back before waving me on in, "sure," he repeats. "Come on in, son."

The trailer is a lot tighter than I had been expecting it to be and there is a smell of fried eggs hanging in the air. A large box on the floor holds a lot of vinyl records - and I mean a *lot*. "I have even more in storage," he says, watching me step over his record collection as he closes the door. "Take a seat there," he says, nodding in the direction of the small couch securely fixed to one of the walls. It's no doubt described as being a two-seater but I take most of it up without assistance. Phil reaches into the baby refrigerator and takes out two bottles of beer before looking at me in a way that makes it clear to see he's wondering if he's being a little too hospitable. "How old are you now?" he asks.

"I'll be seventeen this year," I say.

Phil grins and shrugs his large shoulders. "When somebody asks you that," he says, passing one of the bottles over to me, "you should probably say you're twenty-one."

I smile right back at him and say, "I'll try to remember that." Opening the beer is a little tricky for a second or two with my left hand being so tender but I manage to get the job done. I notice how Phil looks at my bandaged hand but when he opens his mouth like he's intending to ask about it, he soon guides the beer to his lips as if to silence him.

"Boy," he says, "I haven't seen you in years. What've you been up to?"

"Not much. I'm still in High School," I say, "obviously."

"You play much sport?"

"Not much."

"Me neither," he smiles. "My sporting days are long behind me. You dating anybody?"

"Yeah," I nod, "we've been together for a year almost."

"Good," he nods. "She have a name?"

"Eleanor," I reply.

"Eleanor Gayle?"

"Yeah," I nod, wondering just how small the town of Sinclair really is.

"She's a peach," he says, giving me his seal of approval. "I go fishing with her old man. The three of us - me, him and your dad - used to go fishing together. It was never really about the fish we caught," he grins, "which is good because we caught next to nothing! We just used to sit out at the lake and sink a couple of cold ones."

"I don't remember that."

"Must have been too young," he says with a brief shake of the head before returning his bottle to his open mouth. I drink a little of mine. It's not too cold. His refrigerator is either packing up or he has only just got the case of beers home from the store. "I still think of your old man," he sighs but quickly asks afterward, "how're things going for you and your uncle?"

"I don't know," I admit. "He's usually out the house before I've left for school and he comes back a few hours after me."

"So he's working?" he says - making it clear to see that Uncle Nick *was* tossed out of the mill some time ago (leaving me to wonder how long ago and what he's been doing exactly on the days he isn't preaching) or Phil himself left the mill and hasn't spoken with him since. "That's good to know," he says. "What's he doing with himself?"

"I don't know," I say, deciding not to ask him about the mill. "I know he does his preaching from time to time," I blush, "but I don't think he gets paid for that."

"No," Phil says with a grin and another shake of his head, "I don't think he does."

I knock back a little beer to try and gain a little courage. "Mr Delano," I reveal, "the reason I'm here is down to something my uncle said - just a couple of weeks back."

"Oh," he asks - clearly interested, "and what was that?"

"He said you saw my older brother." Phil's face changes to show just how confused he is on hearing that so I try to help him out by adding, "He said you were on vacation and you drove out to visit your daughter at college and you saw my brother in a diner. Or somebody you thought was my brother, anyway."

"Damn," Phil says and he drains his beer before opening the refrigerator to grab two more. Seeing I'm still to finish my beer, he places one bottle atop of the refrigerator and opens the other for himself. "You say your uncle told you that recently?"

"Yes."

Phil shakes his head. This time it's clear for me to see he's doing it out of a sense of disbelief. "Sure," he eventually says, "sure - I remember telling him that. But the thing is," he sighs, "the thing is that happened a couple of years back - maybe more."

The potential lead to find my brother is nothing more than a stone dead trail. My hopes of hearing him apologise for leaving me the way he did, my dreams of him telling me how he'll make up for the lost years... They all crumble to dust.

"I remember thinking it was him at the time," Phil explains, "but the guy said I was mistaken, so maybe I was? I mean - it had been years since I had last seen your brother while I was driving into town, right? Maybe a part of me just wanted to end the great mystery of where he had ended up? And then there's how my own family problems were starting around the same time... Maybe I just wanted to see a friendly face that reminded me of better times, so I made sure I did?"

"Sure," I say before knocking back a little beer, "maybe that's it."

He takes a cigarette from an open pack of Millbrook and lights up. "I'd offer you one," he says, "but it wouldn't sit right with me. I don't want to feel like I'm encouraging you to smoke - what with the damage these things can do."

"It's okay."

"But look," he says - dragging smoke into his lungs, "I'm sorry if I've cancelled your parade here, okay? It could have been your brother I saw but it's just as likely that I was mistaken. The only two people in town who would have been sure one way or the other are you and your uncle, and I told him but he wasn't interested. He didn't even seem pleased to hear how his missing nephew could be okay."

"Yeah," I sigh, "that sounds like Nick." Defeated, I almost entirely drain my bottle of its contents and get to my feet. "Thanks," I say, "thanks. It was good to get an explanation."

"You don't have to go rushing home - you can have another beer, if you want? You could even look through my LP collection and see if there is anything you'd be interested in hearing. Damn," he remembers, "I don't have the stereo here..."

"No," I say on heading for the door, "thanks, but I have to be up early tomorrow."

"Sure," Phil nods. "School, right?"

"Right. One last thing," I say, "where was it you saw him?"

"Your brother? Damn," he answers, "I'm not so sure... It was a long time ago. I could try and remember for you... I could think about it and call the school tomorrow if I remember?"

"Don't sweat it," I say. "You're probably right - it probably wasn't even him."

"I didn't say that."

I step back out into the cold night air, say my goodbyes and start walking. Every couple of seconds, a strong wind rushes along the floor and kicks up swirls of dust and debris but despite the wind, the smell of barbecued meat and shattered dreams refuse to leave. I look back, just the once, to be sure Phil has settled back down indoors but he's still standing there, watching me leave. He tosses his cigarette butt to the floor and waves to me. I nod before turning to carry on walking home.

7

Early morning, I jump out of bed and rush to the window on hearing Uncle Nick leave. I peer out from behind the curtains to get one last glimpse of the man. He's carrying a lunchbox and he isn't wearing his *preaching* shirt, so maybe he does have a job... or maybe he doesn't. Maybe he just wants it to look like he has one. Either way, it means nothing to me. "Good riddance," I say, "you vicious bastard."

It's not even eight a.m. yet. I can't remember the last time I was out of bed this early but I head to the bathroom and carefully remove the cotton bandage from my sore and puffy hand before taking a quick shower. I dress, redress my yet-to-recover hand and head into the kitchen to make myself a cup of coffee and a little breakfast. Uncle Nick's preaching shirt is hanging beside the backdoor, so he must be planning on wearing it again soon. Noticing an open pack of Marlboros and the polished Zippo lighter on the kitchen table, I first decide to help myself to a cigarette, then decide to pocket what remains of the pack. I figure this is my last chance to try and get what is owed to me before I'm gone.

Bringing the smoke into my lungs, I spend at least a minute examining the Zippo. *Daddy* is engraved on one side of it and seeing it is almost enough to bring me to tears. Maybe mom had it done for him when she first found out she was pregnant. It doesn't matter. What matters is I know for certain the lighter belongs to me, the orphaned son, and not the bastard of a baby brother who set out to take over his world after he died.

When I step outside of the family home for the last time, I check the contents of my rucksack just to be sure I have everything I'll need before closing the door behind me. The door locks shut and my keys are on the kitchen table. There is no way back inside for me now unless I force a window open. Walking away from the home, I throw one last look over the rusting Ford on the drive. A lot of fathers work on their cars with their sons as a way of bonding. Uncle Nick left his car to fall apart in front of me, as if trying to convince me I had no way of escaping here.

Lighting another cigarette, I smile, trying to picture how he'll react once he knows I've left him like this. I imagine him not being so fussed - a little angry that I've bettered him this way, but not so fussed until he notices how the Zippo lighter has been taken. I chuckle at the idea of him storming to a nearby store for a packet of cigarettes and a disposable lighter.

The old gal at the bank seems upset about how I want to withdraw all of the money from my account. "You want to close your account?" she asks as if I'm breaking up with her for no good reason.

"That's right," I say. Every small job I've done for somebody in town, every paid errand I've ran, every dollar I've received in a birthday card from some unknown family member... I've always made sure to deposit at least some of it into my account. It wasn't so much of planning for college but more my saving for a deposit on an apartment or something so I wouldn't have to share a roof with my uncle but here I am now, planning on using it to get as far away from Sinclair as I can.

"Are you joining another bank?" she asks.

"No," I smile. "I've decided to be one of those people that keep their money in a sock under the bed."

"Just keeping a little money in your account," she says, "can see you earning interest."

"Fine," I say, deciding she may let me go sooner if I don't close the account today. "I'll leave one dollar in the account - just in case I decide to pay into it again in the future."

The woman's face turns beetroot red, leaving me to wonder if my words just helped her reach that first orgasm in many a year. "That's a very wise head on you, Mr," she stops to get one last look of my name on the slip of paper in front of her, "Lee," and I can't help but picture the mailbox standing beside what is now Uncle Nick's front lawn. THE LEES is stencilled across one side of it. Now he is the only man left standing in that house he claimed as his own, will he change it so it simply reads LEE or what? If I should ever bump into anybody from the town of Sinclair during my travels, I'll be sure to ask them if they know.

"How would you like your withdrawal?" the cashier asks. I tell her I'd like my money - a little over one hundred dollars - in a mixture of tens, twenties and fives. "That's not a problem," she says before she starts counting it out in front of me. She counts it out once and then she double-checks it for me with a smile.

"Thank you," I say, folding the bundle of bills so they can fit inside my back pocket.

"Not a problem," she smiles at me. "Have a wonderful day."

"And you," I say right back at her. Somebody takes my place as soon as I've turned away and the woman who just gave me the keys to freedom probably clean forgets all about me. I'm still thinking about that single dollar I've left here as I walk out of the place, trying to decide whether I should catch a train or a bus to take me away from this town.

8

I RIDE A bus out of Sinclair and to the next town (reason for not getting a ticket further from Sinclair: believing - for some unknown reason - Uncle Nick will try to find me, I figure I'd be easier for a ticket seller to remember if I make it obvious I'm trying to escape the town instead of simply going someplace else for the day) and then board the first train I can without even checking where it's headed. All I know is how it is travelling in the opposite direction to where I've come from. I feel like a kid at school going on a daytrip - looking out of the window and watching fields and towns slipping by. I even hope somebody in the carriage will make polite conversation and ask me *where* I'm headed but nobody does... They pretend to be reading the newspapers they've already read a number of times during the journey instead.

When I finally step off the train, I jump on another bus and I'm so overcome with a sense of optimism that I don't stop to worry about the pretty large bite I've already taken from the little money I have to my name. A much smarter man would have looted my uncle's bedroom drawers for extra funds but what can I say? I'm just a boy...

I climb aboard another bus - briefly holding an old ticket up for the driver to see and he nods his head and I'm travelling again but for free this time. I sneak onto a couple of trains, jumping off when I spot an inspector making his rounds and jump on *one* last bus before arriving in Los Angeles for the first time in my young life.

The city is already growing dark as my ride pulls up at the station. Dark and cold and I have no idea as to where I am. No idea where I can find a cheap room for the night or even a bad job the following morning. With my rucksack over my shoulder, I set off to explore my new surroundings. I know that without shadow of a doubt, what I'm doing right now is the best thing I can do and I'll never regret it. Never.

I examine the newspapers and magazines in a gas station as the Chinese or Japanese clerk watches me, never blinking. Even when I take a cheap energy drink over to the counter, he still looks at me with clear distrust and watches me leave in the same manner - like he's convinced I'll grab the nearest things to the door and run out with them regardless of what they are. The dark gets darker and the cold gets colder. I try to ask a couple of people I pass if there happens to be a hostel or a church nearby but they walk on without listening, convinced I'm asking for loose change or hoping to talk them into joining some up-and-coming suicide cult. I've been in Los Angeles for a couple of hours at most and I've already given up hope on finding a helpful stranger. I head into a park and sit at an empty bench with plans of sleeping there for the night but soon make tracks when a crew of skinheads with a vicious dog appear to be headed in my direction.

The first church I come to, after first spotting its pointed roof against the skyline has been transformed into a rock club. I walk to the door but turn back once a shaved gorilla in a suit blocks my path - soon realising he's done me a favour because I'd only have wasted my money in there. Clean out of other ideas, I return to the bus station I first arrived at and find it to be completely empty apart from the lone ticket seller eating noodles in his booth as he reads a newspaper.

I sit as far away from the booth as possible, hoping to be out of the employee's sight, and push my rucksack under my seat before flicking through an abandoned newspaper I've already read. Old news gets older and more predictable. A car branded with the logo of a private security firm pulls up outside and a man dressed a little like a cop who isn't a cop walks into the station, stopping to hold a conversation with the one remaining employee. Quick as I can, I sneak into the bathroom and hide in one of the stalls. I even drop my pants and sit on the toilet so it'll look like I'm using it if Joe Security comes on in. After some ten minutes, I flush the toilet and wash my hands before returning to the main area. The security guard has disappeared.

Seeing how his car isn't outside, I return to my seat and place my rucksack on one of the chairs. I take one last look around for good measure before lying down, using my collected possessions for a pillow.

It's early morning when I open my eyes. A cleaner is polishing or waxing the floor - I don't stop to ask which of the two it is. I stretch, yawn, throw my bag back over my shoulder and stand on tired legs. The large clock on the wall tells me it's almost six o'clock. Outside, the street is awash with pigeons trying to make the most of their time in charge. A small number of cars pass by but most of the vehicles are those driven by the early-morning street cleaners. I pass the guy cleaning the bus station floors as I leave and we exchange polite grunts by way of greetings. The ticket seller from the previous night isn't sitting in the booth - nobody is. I think about looking into whether the place is hiring on walking back onto the temporarily vacant streets of LA.

9

I GET A good look at my reflection in the mirror on the wall of a public bathroom around midmorning and can't believe how wasted I already look after one night sleeping rough. I have purplish rings beneath my bloodshot eyes, my hair is messy, my clothing crumpled and the rucksack I'm carrying over my shoulder is obviously holding all of my earthly treasures. Despite all of these things, I can't walk so far down most streets without a bum asking me for spare change or a wino temporarily sticking close to my heels as he asks for a little money - *any* money - they claim is needed for their kid's diapers or to pay the electricity bill or buying a coffee and a sandwich. It's obvious for them to see how I don't have shit, but they figure I have at least something more than they have so I should hand it over or forever be a selfish asshole.

I stick to being a selfish asshole and go on walking with my few meagre possessions remaining as my property.

A small store is selling an assortment of bagged doughnuts, six for a dollar. Famished and with only a little bit of my energy drink remaining, I buy six custard-filled doughnuts and carry my purchase out to a nearby park where I sit at a public fountain to enjoy my meal. It isn't long before I have a number of pigeons hanging around my feet so I toss them small chunks of the sweet bread and they gobble it up. "Hey," somebody - a warden or something- calls out soon after, "what's the matter with you? Can't you read the sign?" he asks, drawing my attention to a sign that clearly reads:

DO NOT FEED THE BIRDS.

The man is a couple of inches smaller than me and a couple of pounds lighter than me but the power of maintaining order in this little old park has clearly gone to his head or he has a black belt in karate he'd just love to put to the test. When he realises I'm in no rush to answer him and the pigeons are still chasing one another for scraps of food near my feet, he decides he has no other option but to go on talking.

"The sign says that for a reason," he explains. "Pigeons aren't supposed to eat stuff like that… It isn't a part of their natural diet. Causes all kinds of problems for them - not to mention it encourages them to carry on coming here and making a mess of everything."

I wonder what event in the man's life has led him here. Was it a fondness of John Wayne films when he was a kid but he couldn't make it into the police academy, or did he just take the one job he could find and now he's trying to be the best there is at whatever he does in the name of putting food down on the table? Thinking to myself, I carry on looking at him and reach inside the bag for another doughnut. The pigeons are getting so excited by my movements that they're hovering around me, getting closer and closer, and making noises that encourage their friends to come and join in the fun.

"That's it," the man says on pulling a small notepad and pencil from his pocket, "that's it," he says with a shake of the head. "I'm going to see to it that you get a fine for this. What's your address?" he asks. "Come on," he says when I don't answer him right away. "Name and address- what are they?"

I take a big bite from the doughnut, chew it a little and ask with my mouth full, "You have any identification?"

"What was that?" he asks. "What did you just say?"

"Identification," I repeat. "You want my details, I'm going to have to ask for some identification."

"Right," he smirks, dropping his hands to his hips and grinning to the side of him like he has some invisible friend standing right there. "I'm dealing with a lawyer or something?" he asks. "Am I dealing with some hot-shot prosecutor here - is that it?"

I swallow the chewed food and, despite my hunger, take to tearing what remains of the doughnut I'm holding and scattering it at my feet, driving the pigeons wild. They're jumping on my feet and everything in a bid to get a little food. "I want to know what gives you the authority," I tell him, "to come over to me when I'm just sitting here in the park and start threatening me with fines."

"But that's it," he says, "you're not just 'sitting here in the park', are you? You're feeding the pigeons despite how I've already given you *one* verbal warning!"

"You're giving me a warning?" I laugh. A young mother pushing her child through the park happens to be passing by and she glances at the two of us before deciding it best to move on or risk getting involved. Personally, I think she has made the right choice.

"No," he says, "I *gave* you a warning but you chose to ignore it. Look at this mess," he continues, "looks like we have a petting zoo out here or something!"

I laugh at that but decide enough is enough and the time has come for me to make tracks, so I get to my feet and the pigeons rush back what with my moving and it's either having the birds rush in his direction or seeing me stand that has the man take a step back with a look of panic on his face. I try to hide my feelings of superiority, witnessing just how big a coward the man really is and I toss my bag over my shoulder and walk away from the scene without offering him a second glance.

"Don't let me catch you here again," he shouts after me, "and I'll forget all about your fine."

10

Out of the three churches I visit with hopes of finding a place to stay for the night, two of them have the doors securely locked from the inside to refuse entry to those in need (go figure). The doors of the third church stand wide open and on approaching, I hear the sound of a choir singing from inside and wonder if maybe I should wait for them to finish and come back later, but I walk right in anyway. I don't see anybody as I enter, anybody at all, and the place is nowhere near large enough for a large group of people to hide so well. Walking around the room with saints and angels looking down at me from on high, I notice how the singing is actually louder in one or two places and realise it's a recording that I can hear and wonder if it's actually used as a burglar deterrent or something. And maybe the singing does deter burglars, but it clearly isn't deterring something else... The whole place has a smell of stale cat piss or something about it. In the end I take a seat at a pew and sit there in silence for a while, hands out in front of me.

The church Father eventually comes out from behind a closed door and, not realising he has company, takes to lighting candles to the side of the altar. I try being polite; I try waiting until he has all of the candles he wants burning brightly, but he's taking so long I give up on the idea and make my way over to him. He hears my footsteps when I'm just a metre or so away from him and he turns to look at me from over his shoulder, smiles and nods once, and then he turns back to the candles he's busy lighting. "Excuse me," I ask, "Father...?"

"How can I help?" he asks.

"Well," I say, "this is a little complicated but I'm new to Los Angeles. I have next to no money on me and I have no place to stay. I've already slept rough when I arrived here last night."

"Oh," he says, "you don't have the money to return home?"

"Well, that's just it," I tell him, "I can't return home."

"You're in trouble?"

"Something like that," I say, "but I haven't done anything wrong. That's the reason why I left home in the first place."

He stops lighting his candles and turns to face me with a weak grin and watery eyes. After a moment he says, "The best I can do for you is tell you to return home."

"No," I laugh, "it really isn't."

"Well," he asks, "what can I do for you?"

"You could give me the name of a hostel," I suggest, "or you could even let me stay here for a while - just a few nights, maybe. I'll earn my stay. I'll clean the place up, hand out leaflets, anything."

He smiles at me. "The hostel I know of," he says, "you'd have to prove you're from Los Angeles and you would have to prove your reasons for being unable to return home. A policeman to say you're at risk, something like that."

"Well," I say, "that's not very helpful for a lot of people now, is it?"

"I'm sorry," he says, "but I don't make the rules."

"But what about here?" I ask him, "Can't you let me stay here until I have somewhere else to go?"

"I'm sorry," he says, "but I can't permit you to stay here. I can give you some food tokens, tell you where to find a soup kitchen, but I can't allow you to stay here."

I ask, "Why not?"

Still smiling, the Father says, "I'm afraid this isn't that kind of church."

"*That* kind of church," I laugh. "Did I tell you my whole reason for being out on the streets is down to a religious man?"

"No," he says, "you did not."

"Well it is. It's all down to a man who took to wearing a black shirt with a dog collar so he could preach the words of the Bible. That man," I add on holding my bandaged hand up in front of his face, "took a knife to my hand to teach me God's love and understanding as best as he can see it."

"There's a police station not too far from here. If you go there now and make a statement, I could maybe find a place for you to stay the night."

"I don't believe this," I say. "What about sanctuary? What if I go and claim sanctuary here?"

"Then I would have to inform the police," he answers, "and they would come and take you away as soon as your time was up."

"Jesus," I shout, "I don't believe this!"

"I'm sorry I can't be of any help -"

"No," I interrupt, "it's you don't *want* to be of any help! What's the matter with you," I ask him, "am I too old? Boy comes over to you with no one around and says he can't return home and you *don't* want to offer him a place to stay for the night?"

"I don't know what you mean by that."

"Sure you don't," I say on turning to leave, "sure you don't - you child molesting fuck."

"Jesus!" I hiss once I'm back outside. Filled with anger and with nowhere else to go, I make my way back to the park knowing I'll more than likely kill the supposed warden if he's there and he gets up in my face again. But he isn't there, or he's in another area. The park is reasonably busy because the sky is a clear blue and the sun is shining. Some people are even on the grass, hoping to get a decent suntan, so I sit on the grass just to blend in and take the newspaper from my rucksack so it looks like I'm just here to kill a little time.

After a little while I close the newspaper like I'm done reading it and fold it in half before placing it on the ground to use as a pillow. I don't know who I'm scared is going to see me out here, but I try my best to make it look like I'm only going to be here for a short while... I try to make it look like I'm just on my lunch break or something and I'm trying to catch a suntan before it's time to head back to the nearest college.

11

I WAKE UP after catching a couple hours' worth of sleep and look at my wristwatch. It's early evening and the sun will be setting soon. Despite sleeping through much of the day, I'm still feeling tired and I put that down to my only just waking or my not eating enough. I drink what's left of my energy drink, eat a doughnut and get back on my feet. I brush grass from my back as best as I can, hurl my rucksack back over my shoulder and start walking again. The park is relatively empty now - just a group of joggers, a small number of people out walking their dogs and an even smaller number of people laughing as they play with a Frisbee.

Walking out of the park, I don't see the man who had threatened me with a fine earlier on in the day. Now that I think about it, I realise it's more than likely he wasn't a real warden but just some grifter trying to con new arrivals out of a little money.

A small record store is the perfect place to kill a little time and I find one easily enough. Squashed between two larger stores and without the money to pay for a bright sign like those of its rivals, I almost walk right by the place but notice it just in time.

Rotating fans on the ceiling have strands of cassette tape tied around the blades and I spend a little time thinking about the tapes that have been destroyed for that decoration while I'm making my way through the vinyl records (maybe it's down to being from Sinclair, but this is the first time I've entered a record store that even sells vinyl nowadays) before making my way to the CDs.

I wonder if the cassettes that were destroyed were just stock the manager couldn't sell or whether it was more than that - like they were his ex-girlfriend's favourite tapes or were they the demo-tapes the manager recorded with his band when he was younger? I look up at the clerk - a middle-aged man in a baseball cap and T-shirt who is placing stickers on each CD he takes from a large box to the left of him. I consider asking him about it before changing my mind and carrying on with my casual browsing. The numerous vinyl records are in alphabetical/chronological order and that makes it harder for something to just jump out at me because my mind is trying to think of something good for each section and largely coming up blank.

"Hey," I call out as a thought comes to mind. The clerk stops his pricing and looks at me with indifference. "You don't sell cassettes," I say, "but you stock vinyl."

"And?" he shrugs.

"Cassettes came *after* records," I say as if he wouldn't know already. "Why don't you sell cassettes and get rid of the records?"

"Cassette tapes suck," he says like it's gospel. "They always have and they always will. I was glad to see the back of the little fuckers."

"You can play them in a car," I tell him, "and they've a better sound quality than records."

"Right," he smirks, "you can play cassettes in the car... If you're Amish! As for the sound quality of vinyl records - it all depends on how good a record player you own. Not that many people have one these days. But the people that do," he says, "will always pay good money for a record they want. Mark my words," he says, returning his attention to the box at his side, "the CD is already marching to the end of the road but records will always have serious collectors."

I don't try and talk with him again. I work my way through the records and over to the CDs before leaving. Heading out the door, I look over at him to say goodbye but he's too busy typing away at his computer to notice. Or he pretends to be, anyway.

I cross the street and buy a cheeseburger and fries with a soft drink at the local McDonald's before slowly making my way back to the bus station. It's pretty busy so I blend in easily enough and reclaim the seat that can't be seen by whoever is working the booth that night. The people around me disappear one by one or in small groups until I'm all alone again. Struggling to stay awake, I smoke a cigarette before deciding now is as good a time as any to catch a little sleep. First I drop the end of the cigarette to the tiled floor and then I step down on it before sinking a little lower into the chair, closing my heavy eyelids.

"Hey," somebody says, kicking my right foot to pull me from my peaceful slumber. I sit up feeling alarmed, look all around me to try and remember where I am before noticing the private security guard from last night standing in front of me. I even manage to look beyond him, to his car parked out front of the station. "Hey," he asks me, "what're you doing here?"

"I'm…" I say, panicking already as no words come to mind and my throat is as dry as the planet Mars. "I'm waiting," I tell him, "I'm waiting for a bus."

"Yeah?" He wants to know, "What bus is it you're waiting for?"

"It's… It's the…"

"Is that *your* bag?"

I look to my rucksack and then look back at the guard. "Yes," I nod.

"Pretty full," he observes. "I take it you're waiting for the two-seventy-five?"

"Sure," I say, "that's the one I'm waiting for. The two-seventy-five."

"Son," the guard reveals, "there is no two-seventy-five." He's obviously pleased as hell at how he's outsmarted me. He thinks he's hiding the pride he's feeling but he isn't. Not even slightly.

"Did I say two-seventy-five?" I ask with a boyish grin. "Must be real tired," I say. "It's not the two-seventy-five I'm here for-"

"You have a ticket I can see?" he interrupts.

"Ticket?"

"Yeah," the guard says, "show me your ticket."

I consider buying a ticket, any ticket, just to get him off my back but I don't want to spend any money unless I really have to. "Come on," I say, hoping to reason with him, "I'm new in town and I just need a place to spend the night."

"What do I look like," he asks, "your daddy?"

"I hope not," I tell him, "my old man is dead."

My words don't bother him. They don't bother him because

everybody and anybody will tell you a family member is dead or they have one of many mental ailments to stop you being a wise-ass. It's obvious this has been said to the guard more times than he can recall because he immediately says, "Well I guess you're going to have to call a friend. Come on," he insists, "up and out."

"Look-"

"Up and out," he repeats, kicking at my foot for the second time. "This ain't no hotel. Up and out," he says, "up and out."

"Fucking asshole," I say, getting to my feet and I'm walking to the exit with him right behind me. As we pass the ticket-seller in his transparent booth, the guard points at me and says, "Recognise this clown's face, would you? This pecker-head tries to come back in here, you call me and I'll come get rid of him."

"Pecker-head," I laugh, walking back onto the street. The air is sharp and the sidewalk is wet from a recent rainfall I clearly slept through. I can either walk straight ahead or turn left or right. Seeing as the right offers me a downhill slope and the left offers an uphill struggle, I opt for heading right.

Lighting a cigarette, I can't help but chuckle softly to myself. "Pecker-head," I say once more.

12

A GENTLE RAIN starts to fall but stops almost immediately. The air is the worst thing about being outdoors; it isn't a windy night but the air is real cold. I walk into a couple of convenience stores just to try and get warm but I don't stay long enough in any of them. Because it's late, the employees on duty tend to be college students hoping to get a little reading done but their stoner friends have decided to pay them a visit. Just hearing the shit they talk about is enough to have me back on the streets and I find myself sitting on a low wall despite how wet it is. "Fuck," I say, lighting a cigarette. I regret not exploring LA during the day. If I'd done that instead of sleeping through it, I could have gotten a feel for a larger area... Could have scoped out the quieter areas from the ones where I could find myself getting a kicking if I'm there after dark.

Lighting my second cigarette, I see the holy man heading in my direction. He's dressed in black from head to toe, leather jacket open to show the off-white dog collar around his throat. I put his gloves down to the cold weather and wonder where it is he's heading to at this hour because I can't recall seeing a church or hostel nearby. As he gets closer, I realise he isn't as old as I first assumed he would be; I put him between thirty and forty. The mop of dirty blond hair and few days' worth of stubble have me guess that, like my Uncle Nick, maybe he's just another preacher with a little too much appreciation for the communion wine.

But I'm desperate and I can't see any other potential opportunities on the horizon.

Drawing closer, he realises I'm looking at him and he stares at me for a while but then walks past me like it doesn't matter much to him. "Fuck it," I mutter before loudly saying, "Excuse me, Father?" He stops in his tracks but he doesn't turn to face me - not yet - and I get the feeling he's struggling to decide on whether he should try and help just one more soul tonight or give it all a rest until tomorrow morning finally arrives. But because he hasn't turned to face me I ask, "Reverend?"

"You got it right the first time," he says turning to face me. Only now do I notice how scuffed and beaten his shoes are looking. "What is it you want?" he wants to know.

"Peace on Earth," I smile, "but I'd settle for a place to spend the night if you have one."

He smirks, looks me up and down. "It depends," he says.

I ask him, "On what?"

"Whether you're willing to make a contribution."

"Sure," I say, still smiling. I get to my feet and reach inside my back pocket. The money I have left is still folded in a bundle, so I have to take it all out and try to fish a five out without him noticing the tens or the twenty. I take a step closer and ask, holding the money out for him to accept, "Is this enough?"

"Sure," he says taking the five. He slips it into his pocket on asking, "You have a spare cigarette?"

"Yeah," I say, extracting one from the pack and holding it towards him, "here."

"Thanks," he says and I take the Zippo from my pocket and get a flame going until the cigarette is burning away unaided. "Appreciated," he says. "What's your name?"

"Lee."

"Lee," he repeats. "I knew somebody called Lee, just a few years back."

"He look anything like me?"

"I can't remember. Come on," he says, "follow me."

I fall in at his side. "So what's your name?"

"Father Doyle," he replies. "So where are you from," he asks, "Lee?"

"Far from here," I smile. "Arrived here yesterday."

"Yeah," Doyle says, "it's pretty obvious."

"It is? How?"

"You look like you've not long got out of bed and you're carrying everything valuable you own in that rucksack."

"You got that pretty quick. You ever thought of being a private detective?"

"I don't know," he says. "Maybe."

"Father Doyle," I say to try and prevent an uncomfortable silence falling between us. 'So where's your church?" I ask, "Do we have far to walk?"

"You're already in it," he says with a grin. Smoke comes from his mouth as he talks but it could just be his breath made visible by the cold.

13

I can't help but notice how the neighbourhoods Doyle takes me through are getting crummier and crummier. Windows are barred and front doors have padlocked gates in front of them. Some cars sit on piles of bricks and others are just blackened shells of things long destroyed by fire. The cars that go untouched probably belong to a dealer or somebody who works for a dealer. At the very least, they belong to somebody who the dealer acknowledges in passing and now people won't touch their car because they're not sure just how much the local tough guy likes the owner.

Doyle asks me, "What do you think of Los Angeles so far?"

"I thought it would look better," I say. "No offence."

"None taken. The movies and TV producers want you to think it's all clean and practically everybody is driving a fancy car when they're not sipping cocktails in their pool. Don't get me wrong," he says, "I can show you that side of it, but there are more people struggling nearby than there are taking it easy. You haven't come out here to find fame and fortune, have you?"

"No," I say, "I just had to get away from it all."

"Good. Not *good* that you were having problems," Doyle explains, "just good that you didn't come out here expecting miracles. Los Angeles is a big place," he says, "and like all places, it has more than enough people who've given up on their dreams. Be a realist and everything will turn out fine for you."

I tell him, "I'll try and remember that."

We've been walking so long I'm wondering whether he's hoping I'll grow tired of following him and make my excuses, but I remember the money I've given him and decide to stick it through unless he offers a refund. "Come in here a minute," he says, leading the way into a convenience store, "I need to buy a packet of cigarettes."

"The doors won't be open this late," I tell him but the automatic doors do their job.

"We should've put a bet on it," he grins and the black employee manning the desk, alone glances up at us before looking back down at his magazine. Doyle walks down one aisle and stops to look over the magazines. I stand close to him as he does this. Doyle picks up a music magazine and starts thumbing through it. "Man," he laughs, "have you seen this guy?"

Doyle holds the magazine open for me to see a pale man with long blue hair. He's wearing black lipstick and a torn nurse's uniform (not a real nurse's uniform but the kind a porn star will wear in a skin-flick). A brown leather belt has been tied around his left bicep and in his right hand the man holds a filthy syringe out for the reader to see. Written across the page in bold letters: LET'S GO TO WARR!

"Who is he?" I ask.

"Tony Warr," Doyle says. "He's the latest in a long line of shock-rockers. Can't see him lasting as long as Alice Cooper," he adds with a shrug, continuing to thumb through the magazine. "Alice will outlive us all," he mutters to himself.

"You think he's a bad influence?" I ask for no other reason than to keep the conversation going a little while longer.

"I'm no sociologist," Doyle says as he returns the magazine to its rightful place. "Take a look around," he says, "that's what I'm about to do."

I pick up a magazine and pretend to read it but every once in a while, I lift my eyes just to be sure Doyle hasn't left me high and dry. He eventually makes his way to the counter and buys his cigarettes. As he makes his way back to me, I pretend to be engrossed in the magazine I'm holding. "You buying that?" he asks.

"No," I say on putting it back where I found it. "You done here?"

"Sure," he says with a nod, "let's go."

We walk back into the cold night and Doyle peels the cellophane from his cigarettes. He takes one from the pack and lights it with a disposable lighter he must have purchased back in the store but he doesn't ask if I'd like a smoke. I refuse to light one of my own because of this. I don't want him to know how I actually want a cigarette. "Here," he says and he pulls a Mars bar from one of his pockets and hands it to me.

"Thanks," I say. After a second I tell him, "I didn't see you buy this."

Doyle smirks at me. "I didn't," he admits. "You want to know the best thing about the clerical collar?" he asks. "Nobody ever expects you to steal."

I look to the candy bar, to Doyle, to the candy bar and back to Doyle. "Is this a test of some sort?"

"What do you mean?" he asks, still smiling.

"I don't know," I say. "It's just... You know- the Ten Commandments?"

"Issued in a different time. You think Jesus never stole food? Sure he did. Everybody was stealing. They still are. But Jesus," he says, "you really think he'd agree with capitalism? If you do, you haven't read the Bible. Jesus was a socialist."

"I don't see what that has to do with stealing a candy bar."

"I took it," Doyle says, "because I imagine you are hungry. Are you hungry?"

"Yes," I nod.

"So do you think Jesus would honestly care that I didn't hand under a dollar over to a multi-million dollar business just to end your hunger?"

"I don't know," I shrug. "If everybody thought like that, we wouldn't have any multi-million dollar businesses."

"The rich can't enter Heaven. I'm just trying to help my fellow man out."

14

WE'RE WALKING DOWN a street that somehow manages to be more dilapidated than the last. First every other streetlight has been broken by vandals, then every two. Abandoned factories stand here and there - corpses people have forgotten to bury. I know it's the two-storey building that Doyle is leading us to; a two-storey building that leads back quite a stretch and is surrounded by tall grass - the only patch of green land I've seen in quite a time. The windows on the first floor have been boarded up but the windows on the second haven't, so each and every one has been broken by kids with stones. As we get closer to our destination, I finally make out what's written in tall letters above the double doors at the front.

SAINT CLAIRE'S ELEMENTARY SCHOOL.

Doyle asks me what I find so funny. "Saint Claire's," I tell him. "Doesn't sound so different to where I'm from."

"Maybe it's a sign," he says as we approach the entrance.

I say, "You're not a real Father, are you?" but continue following him anyway. It's not like I have anyplace else to go or anybody else to put my faith in.

Doyle stops and says, "Sure I am. Was Jesus recognised in his time? No, and look at what happened to him. Poor guy had to rise from the dead just to be taken seriously by enough people."

"I didn't mean to upset you," I tell him, "and I'm grateful for you giving me a place to stay... Even if it is more than a little rundown."

Doyle smiles. "Don't let the way it looks fool you," he says. "Building has working electricity - but I reckon it's best you only turn on the lights in a few rooms so you don't attract any unwanted attention - and running water. It even has gas in the science labs but I haven't found a reason to use any of that yet."

I look beyond him and say, "You're kidding me, right? Why would they let this place have all of that?"

Doyle says, "I'd love to say it's just a shining example of how the Lord provides to those in need, but I have other suspicions. Anyway, come on in and I'll give you a guided tour. Make sure you wipe your feet on the way in," he adds and I think he's only joking until I see how he wipes his feet on the mat in front of the door so I follow suit.

"So do you have a key for this place?"

Doyle pushes one of the doors open and smiles at me. "Don't need one," he says. "The lock was broken a long time ago. Only the back is still locked up pretty secure."

I ask him, "Did you break the lock?"

"Please," he smirks, "I'm a man of God. Anyway, follow me."

I follow him inside, down a long and narrow corridor with doors on either side that lead into long abandoned classrooms. There's a faint smell of mould and mildew hanging around but the broken windows on the next floor must let enough air into the place to stop it from getting too bad. There are dead leaves on the floor, a couple of torn and crumpled newspaper pages but next to no other litter. The lockers once claimed by children are all standing open, some have been violently forced open and there's a little graffiti on the walls that I can just about make out in the sparse moonlight.

I ask, "Do you share this place with many others?"

"Nah," he says, leading me further down the corridor. I glance in every room we pass, just in case a crazed murderer is waiting to get a drop on us or a couple of dealers have taken to making crystal meth on the premises but then I remember what he said about the science lab having working gas and I realise if dealers were going to claim any part of the building, it would have to be the science lab. "I'm the only guy that stays here full time," he reveals. "People drop by, but they come and go. Hardly anybody stays longer than the one night."

"Do kids ever come in here?"

"No," he laughs, "they didn't want to come here when it was open, so why would they want to come here now that it's closed?"

"I don't know," I shrug, "to wreck the place, maybe."

"If kids come to take a look inside, it's during the daylight hours. No kid wants to be trapped in a place that could be filled with bums. You remember what a youngster's imagination is like, surely?"

"I guess."

Doyle stops for a moment, just to turn and ask me, "How old are you, Lee?"

"Twenty-one."

"Sure," he grins. "Right. Anyway," he says on turning back around, "let's keep on walking. As you can probably tell already, this corridor is filled with empty classrooms. The main hall is right at the end of the corridor and you can help yourself to an old gym mat to sleep on. Through those doors," he says with a point, "stairs leading upstairs. There's nothing really of interest up there; science lab and a library but all the books and computers are long gone. I'm sure you'll recognise the toilets," he continues as he starts walking once more, "by the little matchstick man or lady on the door. Oh, and there's a kitchen," he adds, "if you go into the hall and take the door to the left. They took the ovens but the refrigerator is still here; thank the Lord."

15

I FOLLOW DOYLE into the kitchen area and he turns on the lights. The smell of abandonment is pretty bad in here but I'm too impressed by the working electricity and the sight of a refrigerator that belongs in an army base or something it's that big. "Did I mention the working kettle?" Doyle asks approaching the refrigerator, that *huge* refrigerator.

"No," I say, "you didn't," and I lean back against a worktop but quickly take a step away from it noticing what has to be rat or mice droppings.

"Well," Doyle says opening the refrigerator, "I have one. I bought it myself," he says, taking it out from - you guessed it - the refrigerator. It's soon joined by two mugs, a small bag of sugar, a teaspoon and a small jar of store-brand instant coffee. "You might think it a little crazy," he says, "keeping all this in here, but there is a reason."

"I'm sure there is."

"Rodent infestation," he says. "I keep things in the refrigerator so they can't run all over them. Don't worry, I clean everything before putting them in there."

I ask, "You have cockroaches?"

"Not that I've seen. I reckon the mice or the rats eat them. How many sugars do you take in your coffee?"

"Two," I say, "if you don't mind."

"Not at all," Doyle assures me, "not at all. A lot of people are trying to cut sugar out of their diet," he tells me on preparing us both a cup of coffee while he waits for the water to boil, "but they shouldn't and I'll tell you why. Have I ever told you about my dad?" he asks like we're old friends who've just happened to bump into one another after some years.

"No," I reply, lighting a cigarette, "I don't think you did."

"Dad," he says, "was in the army. Nothing worth talking about; he wasn't special ops or anything like that, he was just your regular private. But he tells me about this one training exercise he went out on when I was just a boy. Him and his group," Doyle says, "they have to drop so much weight on this exercise and they all decided they could go without sugar. I mean, you can put up with a couple cups of coffee without sugar, can't you?"

"I reckon so."

"That's what they thought," Doyle says as the water in the kettle begins to boil. "But they all ended up getting tired and cranky, more so than they usually do on these exercises Uncle Sam likes to put them through. It was not having sugar," he smiles. "That was the whole point of the exercise, you see? Sometimes you'll think something isn't so important and that you can do without it, but you can't. Makes you think some, doesn't it?"

"Yeah," I say with a nod, "it does."

"Sugar," he smirks. "Dad loved telling me that story, especially when I was at an impressionable age... No wonder I take five in my coffee."

"You're kidding?"

"Cross my heart."

"Won't that be a little too much for your teeth to deal with?" I ask him.

"One day," Doyle tells me, "when I was just a young boy, too young to even remember it well, my parents were really worried because they didn't know where I was. They checked everywhere, called everybody. You know where they found me? The pantry. I was in the pantry, eating from a bag of sugar. Two bags I'd already helped myself to were at my feet. My teeth started dropping out the very next day."

"Seriously?"

"Seriously," Doyle says and to prove his point, he takes his hand to his mouth and slips out the dentures he's wearing. He must have three or four teeth in total that are his own and he grins at me so I get a good look at his bright pink gums before slipping his dentures back into his mouth. "I lost one or two when I got older, fighting and such, but you get the idea."

"Sure," I nod, "I get it."

He pours boiling water into the cups, stirs the contents of them both and hands one over to me. I thank him but make sure to ask, "You haven't given me the one with five sugars in it by mistake, have you?"

Doyle laughs and lights one of his own cigarettes. "I guess I'll find out later," he says, "if you're crawling up the walls all night!"

From somewhere deep inside the building, I hear two loud bangs and they cause me to jump out of my skin but Doyle acts like he didn't hear a thing. They didn't sound like gunshots but they sounded a lot like somebody was taking a sledgehammer to one of the walls. "Fuck," I chuckle through nerves. "What was that?" I ask.

"Won't be nothing," Doyle answers me with a casual shake of his head. "You hear a lot of bumps in the night around here; plumbing complaints that are going ignored, old cupboards or blackboards dropping from the walls. When you've been here as long as I have," he says, "you come to recognise them as the sound of Saint Claire's beating heart. To Saint Claire," he adds, raising his coffee in the air like he's making a toast at a fancy party.

"To Saint Claire," I repeat back to him.

Doyle takes a mouthful of coffee and shudders for a fraction of a second after he swallows it. "Come on," he says, "we'll go and get you a mat to sleep on and then we'll find you a room for the night."

I ask, "What should I do if somebody comes into my room during the night?"

"I don't know," he says, "it depends."

"Depends on *what?*"

"Well, if it's a sweet young virgin with a pair of gravity-defying tits who'd like you to teach her how to make love, I'd go teach her how to make love as best as I can remember it."

"And if it isn't?" I laugh.

"Then I'd be sure to take the guy's money before I take off my pants."

16

I'm NOT ONE hundred per cent sure that I've been catching any sleep because there is no clock for me to take the time from, but I'm pretty sure I keep getting woken up. First it was a gentle rain that sounded like somebody was drumming his fingers along the boards that cover the windows and then - and this probably was just a dream - it was the sounds of somebody trying to pull those boards loose. I keep feeling like somebody is watching me from the darkest corner. Every single time I get an itch, I jump up and pat myself down just in case it's an insect of some kind crawling all over me, looking for an orifice to lay eggs in.

So I walk out of the deserted classroom and step out into the hallway. Seeing a faint light coming from the room across the hall - the room Doyle went into - I head on over to the door and tap on it. Through the small window high up the door, I can already see him. He's sitting on the floor with his back against the wall, a blanket over his legs and his gloves removed as he reads what I imagine to be the Bible. The light is coming from a desk lamp he has on the floor beside him. He doesn't look up right away, so I wait a second or two before knocking a little louder. Doyle looks towards the door (he probably won't be able to make my face out from the darkness) and invites me in with a wave of his right hand. I give a sigh of relief before entering. "Lee," he says, closing his book. "Are you okay?"

"Sure," I say, noticing how he has pushed all of the useless desks to one side of the room and stacked all the chairs to give himself a little extra space. There's an old gym mat on the floor with a torn and dirty sleeping bag on top of it.

"I just can't get to sleep," I add on lighting a cigarette. I toss him one to try and make up for my intruding like this.

"What's the point of having a place to stay," Doyle asks, "if you can't get to sleep there?" I wait for him to be lighting his cigarette before answering him. "I'm just not used to sleeping in a place like this," I claim. "Los Angeles is a big place and that means it has a large police force. What if a bunch of cops come in here to poke their noses around?" A split second before his cigarette is burning away and he allows the flame of his lighter to die out, I catch a brief glimpse of his tattoo. It looks to be a letter on each knuckle.

"We're not causing any trouble here," he says, "and even if they did come on in here to arrest us, the worst that would happen is we spend a night in the cells and get a cooked breakfast before they toss us back out." He blows a couple of smoke rings from the back of his throat before looking back at me to ask, "Where was it you said you're from?"

"Sinclair," I tell him.

"That's funny," he says, "it does sound similar to this place. But what's it like there?" he asks. "How're things in the town I'd never heard of before this minute?"

"Pretty quiet," I shrug. "Most people that are born there stay to die there."

"And you didn't want to be one of them?" Doyle smiles. "You have a girl back home," he says, "or is she out in LA?"

"I had a girlfriend," I tell him, "but we broke up."

"So you ran away so you'd never have to see her again, is that it?"

"No," I say, "it was me who ended it. But anyway," I go on, just to change the subject, "what's that tattoo on your hand?"

Doyle looks at it for a second like he'd forgotten clean about it. "Oh," he smirks, "take a gander," he says and with the cigarette hanging loosely from his lip, he makes two fists and holds them out so the thumbs are touching. The ink he's had scarred onto his hands? It spells out REDEEMER.

"Neat," I say. I'd have said it was pretty funny but I don't know him from Adam, not really, and I don't want to risk offending him. "Do you have any others?"

"Couple on my arms," he says, "one or two on my chest... I forget. Most of them are army-related."

"You served in the army?"

"Nah," he says with a shake of his head and then when he

pulls on his cigarette, I remember all about mine and drag a little smoke into my own lungs. "There was a tradition of Doyle men being in the army, but they wouldn't let me join. Some test results said I had violent tendencies or tendencies of violence, I forget which. How stupid is that?" he smirks. "The army is rejecting men because they find them to be a little violent!"

"Yeah," I nod in agreement, "I can't say that makes any sense to me."

"But what about you," he asks- bringing the subject back onto me, "you in the army? Twenty-one years of age," he whistles. "I could be sitting with a hardened killer."

"No," I smile, shaking my head. "I've never been in the army."

Doyle laughs again. "Funny," he says. "You make a point of saying you've never been in the army but you don't deny you're a killer."

"Would a killer be creeped-out," I ask, "staying in an old school?"

"If he sees the faces of all his victims looking back at him from the shadows," Doyle says, "I bet you he would be."

17

I've been staying with Doyle at Saint Claire's Elementary for little under three months now because he hasn't asked me to leave so I don't and he doesn't seem to mind me following him around. I think he even enjoys the steady company, but I've been staying with him for little under three months and I already feel confident that should anybody from Sinclair happen to take a vacation in Los Angeles and run into me, they would struggle to recognise me. The puppy fat I was carrying has fallen clean off. I'm wiry now but stronger than I've ever been. More alert, too. I look back at that first night in Saint Claire's - that first night when I stayed in Doyle's room until morning because I was scared, and feel something like shame.

Maybe my uncle would recognise me, or feel like he knows me from someplace if he was to see the scar on the palm of my left hand, but that would be all. It was Doyle who took the stitches from my hand when it started to feel funny; when a dull ache took claim of the area of flesh and refused to budge. He took a look at it and said it would be best to take the stitches out before infection set in, so he took a few things from a hardware store and removed the thread himself. He asked about the scar, telling me how the Bible says you should remove your left hand if it offends you before asking if that was why Uncle Nick had punished me the way he had done, but I had to confess to having no idea how the crazy bastard's mind works.

Little under three months without that crazy old bastard breathing down my neck and I couldn't be happier.

In the basement of Saint Claire's, there's a locker room and a shower area from when schoolchildren used to have their Physical Education here so I get to have a hot shower every morning because the hot water is still running. Doyle let me in on *that* secret after a couple of days, saying he hadn't been planning on telling me first because he'd guessed I wouldn't make it through one night. We have quite a lot of towels and whenever we have to, we take a bundle of them to the nearest Laundromat with some clothes. Sometimes we take the items somebody else is washing from a machine and chuck our stuff in if they aren't there, but we mostly just collect the money we find until we have enough because the money I had to my name is long gone. Doyle steals food from the stores easily enough, and you can practically help yourself at the fruit and vegetable sellers with outdoor stalls if you're smart enough. But there are a few people, mostly Italians, who'll gladly offer us a hot meal or a bag filled with groceries if they happen to see us passing. A barber in one neighbourhood is always happy to shave us with his cut-throat razor or trim our hair whenever we want, because he really likes Doyle and so he's taken to me now too

Sometimes, we'll stand outside a number of churches on a Sunday and when the worshippers come walking out, Doyle will start laughing and joking with them and some give him a little money. Other times, Doyle will preach on a street corner and people will drop money at his feet. But truth be told, we only ever seem to spend the money we're given on cigarettes. Cigarettes are near impossible to steal because they're always kept behind the counter.

I suppose my one gripe comes down to clothing. We'll sometimes pick up some clothes that have been donated to a church or we'll go into a charitable place and see if they have anything to give us, and Doyle *always* manages to get something that not only suits him (black jeans or trousers, black shirts) but fits him like it was made especially for him. If it's black, it's his. I know, I know, I left home with all of my clothing, but I just can't help but feel a little envious when I see him wearing something that cost him nothing and he still looks great. What's funny though is I have a pair of black jeans, a pair of black trousers and at least one black shirt with me that I took from home, but I haven't even taken them from my rucksack. I don't feel like I can wear them around him because black is *his* thing and although I owe him a lot, I just can't stand the idea of handing him my black clothes and seeing him wear them better than I could ever dream of. I swear to you, even on the few occasions we've swiped clothing from somebody's washing line, Doyle manages to take something black that fits him just perfect.

I tell you, I don't know how anybody with his luck could wind up homeless. He must have made the decision to live the way he does or something. If he didn't, he must be on the run from the law or worse because that is the only explanation I can think of. But even if that is the case, so what? He's been nothing but good to me, he's never threatened me, never got me into any trouble.

I don't care at all what he may or may not have done in his past because I owe him everything.

18

Doyle stubs the cigarette out on the sole of his shoe and drops it into the trash before heading into the drugstore. Sitting at a bus stop right across the street, I watch the door close shut behind him and then I lose sight of him because the front of the drugstore is practically nothing but glass, so the sunlight and whatever else that can reflect brightly off of it is doing just that. I glance down at the cigarette I'm holding between two fingers and see how just under half of it remains. There's no rush, not really, so I take a leisurely pull on it and look back to the drugstore across the street. The drugstore is called LIEFELD AND SONS. The proprietor, Liefeld, I guess is a man approaching old age who is always happy to make conversation with Doyle. Always happy to discuss his young grandson. This is the third time we've dropped by this month but I'm sure it will work again because Doyle is sure it will work again.

I look around me, just to see if there are any faces I recognise but there isn't. I get to my feet, take one final drag on my cigarette and drop what's left of it before heading to the drugstore. Drawing closer, I manage to get a look inside. I only see the top of Doyle's head, because he is browsing behind one of the shelving units. The old man is smiling to himself, smiling at something funny he must have said to Doyle seeing it was him entering the store- and making notes in the black ledger he's so fond of.

The bell above the door rings as I enter and the second the old man raises his head to get a look at me, I clear my throat and stroll on in trying to look as suspicious as I can manage, which isn't too difficult at all. For some unknown reason, the old man has a clear dislike for me. Maybe I remind him of somebody, I don't know… Maybe I'll ask him about it some time, but not *this* time. I'm not looking directly at him but I can see him well enough to know he's frowning already. I turn down one of the small aisles, turn at the end of it to step onto the next and then I crouch down low like I'm looking at something. As bad luck would have it, I'm squatting down in front of the assorted tampons and other items a woman may purchase once a month. Maybe more if she's a particularly heavy bleeder.

I stay down low and pretend to be looking but not touching. I hear the squealing hinges of the small door that leads behind the counter as the old man opens it and comes walking out onto the shop floor, his footsteps loud on the polished tiles. I'm still not looking at him but I hear him taking the long way around, like he's trying to catch me in the act or he's thinking I might try and make a run for it although I've never once rushed out of here yet. The sound of his steps comes to an abrupt end and he asks, "Can I help you, son?"

I look to my right and see him standing at the end of the aisle with his arms folded across his chest. "I don't know," I say to him. "I'm just looking."

Keeping his arms folded, he takes one step forward. His eyes dart to what's in front of me before moving right back on me, like he thinks I might try and pocket something in that one split second his eyes moved away from me. He takes a deep breath- puffing out his chest to try and look intimidating and releases it asking, "You know what those are for, don't you?"

I look to the padded towels and plastic wands with a cotton coating. "Sure," I say.

"Are you looking for any particular brand?" he asks. We've had two conversations almost identical to this one in the last few weeks alone, the first was on hair conditioner and the second was on treatment for a fungal nail infection.

"I don't know," I shrug, slowly turning my head back to the sanitary products. "Which brand would you say is the best?"

"For a man," he asks, "experiencing his period?"

"They're not for me," I smile at him, trying to remember if the last time I was in here was (supposedly) down to my mother or sister or even a girlfriend. "They're for my girlfriend," I add, deciding no mother would send her son in to buy these for her or a sister her brother. "She's a real heavy bleeder," I say, "*torrential*, maybe. One night last month, she came on early. You should have seen the sheets," I sigh, "looked like somebody had been murdered on them."

"I see," he says. "And did your girlfriend ask you to buy something for her this month?"

"No," I tell him, "because if she did, I'd have some idea of what to pick up. But it's just that it's driving her crazy," I say. "Ever since she went on the morning after pill, her bleeding has gotten out of hand."

The small bell above the door sounds. Doyle shouts, "I'll see you soon."

"Yes," the old man says, smiling as he looks over to the door and waves. "Come back again."

His smile has gone and his eyes are back on me a heartbeat before I hear the door closing. I ask him, "What was I saying?"

"Your girlfriend," the old man replies, "is having some difficulty with her birth control."

"That's it," I say, standing. I hear my knee pop but the old man is so startled at me getting to my feet all of a sudden, all he does is take an involuntary step back. He didn't hear the sound of my knee or he'd probably be trying to sell me something for it. "Could you recommend something to help her out? Something that wouldn't have the same effect as what she's using now?"

The old man asks, "Do you know what it is she's being prescribed?"

"No," I say, "I don't think so, but I can find out for you."

"Find out," he says, clearly annoyed to find himself still talking to me when he could be writing away in his ledger. "Better yet," he adds, "bring your girlfriend in next time you're by and I can discuss it with her."

"Okay," I say with a nod, taking quick steps for the door with the old man following me as best he can in case I make a grab for something. "Thanks. You've been really helpful," I finish, walking out onto the street to walk away as quick as I can. I look back over my shoulder, just the once, to see the old man staring at me as he takes cautious steps back into his store. I turn the corner and the old man falls out of sight but Doyle is suddenly walking alongside me, smiling as he brings a cigarette to his lips. "Well," I ask, "did you get anything?"

"A little Valium," he says. "You could do with one right now," he grins, "you look a little tense."

19

THE WIND IS kicking up a real fuss outside, howling like crazy. We're sitting in Doyle's room, smoking a little grass one of the guys who will stay here from time to time left behind for us to enjoy, and everything feels sort of dreamlike to me. Maybe it's the way the lamplight makes the thick smoke look like it's snaking around the room, maybe it's just real good green we've got this time. Despite the mellow high, I can't help but notice the chill in the air. The cold is the only bad thing about Saint Claire's. I don't mention it because I know how it annoys Doyle, his not being able to get the radiators working. He says he's tried bleeding them, tried kicking them, tried moving the dials from *on* to *off* real fast. Says he's even tried swearing at them in three languages but they just refuse to heat up.

"I ever tell you," I ask without knowing I was planning to, "that *fanny* means *pussy* over in England?"

Doyle slowly releases smoke from his chest and nods. "I knew that," he says, nodding real slow. "I lived in Britain for a short while."

"Really?" I ask accepting the joint he hands over to me, "How long ago was this?"

Doyle looks up to the ceiling and thinks about it for a second. "I don't know," he says, "five years, maybe longer. You think it's cold here…"

"You stay in London?"

"For a while. I ended up staying further north. The people are friendlier up north. Well, they were to me."

I nod as if in understanding. "Why'd you come back?"

"I didn't want to be one of those people. One of those people," he says, "who move to another country and hate the fact it isn't like home? Fuck that," he says, "if home was so great, you should never have left it. So I moved back here. To the US, I mean. It never changes here. Not really."

Nodding, I pass him the joint back. "I'm going to bed," I say.

"Don't let the bedbugs bite," Doyle says and then he closes his eyes tight and starts laughing, hands covering his eyes. It looks and sounds a little like he's crying but I don't mention it, just in case he is. "Good night, Doyle," I say, walking out of his room on unsteady legs and closing the door behind me to grant him a little privacy. I stand there for a minute to try and get my balance because the corridor is swaying. "Fuck," I say, stumbling to my room. I push the door open and stop because something doesn't feel right with me. I take a deep breath, like I'm thinking a little extra oxygen to the brain will help me see things more clearly, and it works straight away because my eyes lock onto the dark mass on a part of the floor near the corner. The only thing in the corner over there should be the gym mat I sleep on, my rucksack and the table lamp we lifted from a charity store. Not one of those things should make a shape like the one I'm seeing. I press the light switch on the wall even though there isn't a light-bulb in this room. Doyle and me keep talking about getting a couple but we never seem to get around to it and at this moment, I curse myself for that. I curse us both.

I clear my throat and ask, "Anybody here?" After a moment I ask again, a little louder, "Anybody here?"

"This is my room," somebody growls from the corner. "Plenty of other rooms, this is my room."

"No," I say, "this is my room. This is where I sleep."

"Fuck you," the intruder hisses. "My room! This is my room! Take one of the others!"

"This is my room!" I shout. The black patch against the darkness moves and takes the shape of a man climbing to his feet. The grass I'd been smoking earlier hits me hard. I want to run away and hide but my legs have turned to stone as the figure takes confident strides in my direction, shouting so loud it's impossible for me to make out just what it is he's saying. All I can do is hope he doesn't have a knife.

"This is my room!" I shout, trying to make myself look bigger and sound tougher than I really am. Like an idiot, I'm standing right in the centre of the doorway so even if the intruder would

like to leave right now, he can't. "This is my room!" I shout at
him.

<h1 style="text-align:center">20</h1>

I REMEMBER THE two pieces of advice my brother gave me on fighting when I was just a boy. The first piece was how you should *never* fight an ugly person, because they have nothing to lose when you think about it. And his second piece of advice was you should *never* fight a bum. Bums, he explained, were tough because they lived on the streets and so they had to fight to survive. Bums fought for space in a shop doorway that could keep them out of the rain. Bums fought for scraps of food and the last mouthful of alcohol at the bottom of a cheap bottle of wine. Bums fought just for the sake of it.

And bums, he told me, carried whatever weapons they had found or made on their turf.

I'm still shouting, "This is my room!" as the faceless intruder comes at me. I'm shouting because I'm hoping more than anything that Doyle will hear me and come rushing to my aid. I'm hoping just as much that Doyle hasn't passed out in his room or put my screaming down to a grass-induced fantasy.

And I'm wondering if my time on the street makes me tougher than my unexpected opponent. I mean, say he's only in Saint Claire's because he had one too many to drink and so his wife locked the door and he couldn't get in. With him having a nice bed and three warm meals to look forward to the next day, will that make me instinctively tougher? Will my *true* homeless state give me the edge over this imposter? This fake?

I've never had a fight before in my life. Not one. Various kids at school challenged me to one from time to time, sure, but I always talked my way out of it. I talked my way out of it because I was scared that getting into a fight would see the principal calling Uncle Nick in to see him and then he'd go punish me for the day's work he had missed. Now, with a fight looking like the only available option, I don't know what I'm going to do. I don't like the idea of throwing a punch before my rival has thrown one at me first, so my aggressive act is just that… An act.

Still little more than a silhouette, my rival lunges forward and takes a tight hold of my arms. He's trying to restrain me, hoping to push me to the ground I guess, and I can smell cheap alcohol coming from him as he pants. Smells like he's been drinking paint stripper or something just as nasty. And my heart is beating so wild and so much adrenaline is pumping through my veins that I feel like I'm going to pass-out or barf.

"Get off me!" I holler. I bring my head down, trying to head-butt my opponent, but I somehow manage to mess it all up and my left eyebrow takes a knock and the force of impact has my jaw slam shut. I open my mouth to shout again and realise a second too late that my left arm has been released. Still holding onto my right arm, my newfound enemy punches me in the gut. I drop to my knees as the air is knocked clean out of me.

"Pussy!" He shouts, "I'll show you how you put your head in!" and then he brings his forehead straight to my nose. I hear the break and I feel what *has* to be my blood spill across my face, over my mouth, but it doesn't hurt so bad. I put that down to the adrenaline that's still racing around my veins. I'm thinking I'm too pumped-up to register pain but then I feel a clenched fist sock me in the jaw and it dazes me enough to have me drop to my side, the faceless enemy releasing my arm to let me drop at his feet. He starts shouting again but I'm too dazed to hear the start of it.

"Stupid," I catch him shouting at me, "asshole! You want to-"

I'm aware of an insurmountable presence appearing as if from nowhere. It's directly over me and I see two strong arms reach out from the darkness and take hold of my attacker. "Hey!" he shouts in alarm but then he's pulled right over me like he's just a paper bag caught in a tornado and from the corridor behind me, it sounds like somebody is working a punching bag. I taste the blood of mine he spilled as it trickles into my mouth. I realise the blood is still pouring, running to the side of my face and onto the floor. Not wanting a bloodstain I'll forever see on the floor of my room when it's light enough, I force myself into a sitting position and try to gather my thoughts. From the corridor, I can still hear punching sounds. But it doesn't sound like somebody is working a punching bag no more, because the sounds are too wet.

Getting to my feet, I try to shake the cobwebs from my head and finally turn around. After a second, my eyes adjust to the little light available and I see Doyle kicking the shit out of a figure at his feet. Doyle isn't wearing his shirt. Did he take it off especially for this or had he been undressing for bed when he finally heard me?

"Fucking fucker!" Doyle shouts on kicking the man now positioned on the floor at his feet one last time and I notice how my enemy who turned into Doyle's enemy is trying to crawl away. He must think if he stays down low, Doyle will have pity on him and let him get out of here. I try not to think of the intruder staggering home to a wife who unlocks the door because she knows he's hurt. I try not to think of the beating he'll inflict on her to try and grab back some of the confidence that was taken from him tonight.

"Fuck off outta here!" Doyle screams with a wave of his hands, "And if you ever come back, I'll fucking kill you!"

"Here," Doyle says as he takes a hold of my arm, "let's get a proper look at you," he insists on pulling me to his room. I take one last look at the retreating, broken figure as it crawls on and then we're in Doyle's room. The lamp is still on, so I see the blood coming from the split skin over Doyle's knuckles as well as the tattoos he has on his body. A lot of them look like he done them himself, or somebody he trusted did. Doyle takes my face in his hands and looks me in the eye. "You concussed?" he asks me, "Did he stomp on your head?"

"No," I say. "I can see my eyelids," I add, noticing them. "Do I have two black eyes?"

"You sure do," Doyle says, taking a step back as he ruffles my hair. "You've only gone and got your first broken nose. Fucker broke that on you good and proper. We'll go get you cleaned up in a minute."

"I knew it was broken," I sigh. "It doesn't hurt," I say. "How weird is that?"

"Don't worry about it," Doyle tells me, "broken noses can bleed like you wouldn't believe but they never really hurt. It's mostly cartilage," he knowingly grins. "Only broken bones and hearts can hurt."

21

Having finished my morning shower, I turn the faucet until water stops coming from all showerheads and wrap a towel around my waist before walking into the adjoining locker room. I don't know if the kids who came to Saint Claire's were particularly vain or not, but there is a pretty large mirror on the wall of the changing room. I approach it, eyes on my reflection. I wouldn't say my eyes are still black, the swelling has certainly gone, but faint purple/bluish rings are still underneath them. Doyle says all signs of bruising will be gone in a week or two.

Keeping my eyes locked onto my mirror image, I first turn my head to the left and then slowly to the right, getting a good look at my self from a side angle. My nose looks a lot like a beak to me ever since it was broken in the attack. You can't see where the skin had been torn by the force of the intruder's forehead landing against it and the swelling has gone down a lot quicker than it did my eyes, but yeah... My nose is most definitely beak-shaped these days. Doyle said the look gives me added character, that plenty of men considered handsome these days have a nose like mine, that some will pay a good fortune to have it like this, but I know he only said that to make me feel better. That's why I won't mention my nose to him or look at it for too long if he's near.

Sighing, I head over to the bench at the wall holding a long row of hooked pegs. My trousers are hanging from one such peg and the rest of my clothes are as I left them, which is neatly folded on the bench below. I've only just quit taking a chair-leg into the showers with me but as far as Doyle is concerned, I had stopped doing that a long time ago. I didn't want him to know just how much the beating I received had troubled me. He kept telling me the guy responsible wouldn't be coming back, but the basement here can be pretty scary at times as it is.

Sitting down on the bench, I reach underneath it to take

my socks out from my shoes and hear Doyle's whistling as he approaches. Think of the Devil... He walks in naked save for the towel around his waist and the shoes on his feet. The paper bag in his hand will contain one bar of soap, a shaving razor, a small bottle of cologne and body spray. He doesn't stick to using a particular brand of cologne or soap, but he insists on using one body spray and one body spray alone. If we must, we'll go all over the city until we find a store he can lift it from. Not that I'm complaining or anything. I mean, the day after my nose was busted- Doyle went out and got a whole bunch of light bulbs so we'd know straight away if somebody was in a darkened room.

"How's the water today?" he asks with a smile. I still haven't asked him *why* he thinks this place is still receiving electricity, gas and hot water. Truth be told, I'm a little scared to ask in case I jinx the place and we lose all of our privileges because of my curiosity. If something is fine, don't question it. Just accept something is finally working out right for you.

"Fine," I say with a smile, first slipping on my socks, then standing to pull my underwear up my legs.

"That's what I like to hear," Doyle says with a grin, standing just a couple of pegs away from mine as he kicks off his shoes. "You don't have your cigarettes with you, do you?"

"Sure," I nod, delving a hand deep inside my trouser pockets.

"Solid gold," he says, "I left mine upstairs."

Doyle can do this so easily, walk all the way down here with just a towel around his waist to cover his modesty and shoes on his feet to stop them from turning black, but I can't. I try to keep as many of my things around me at all times, just in case somebody turns up out of the blue to tell us we have to leave. And by *somebody*, I mean a gang of men with hammers and such working on behalf of the city council.

"Here you go," I say, handing him my pack of cigarettes and Zippo lighter. He thanks me, lifts one cigarette from the pack and lights it. If he has ever thought about the engraving on the side of the Zippo, he's never mentioned it. Maybe he thinks it's a delicate matter, maybe he thinks I simply found the Zippo. Maybe he thinks it's nothing at all to do with him.

"This Zippo was my dad's," I say returning it to the safety of my pocket.

"Yeah?" He asks, "You have anything else of his?"

"Not that I can think of," I shrug. "But how about you," I ask him, "you have anything of yours?"

"His eyes," Doyle says.

22

Walking through a particularly flash area of LA, Doyle walks into a store so he can pick up some cigarettes and I stand outside where the newspapers are kept. I'm just looking over the headlines, not paying any real attention to them, as Doyle comes out with his purchase and says, "Let's make tracks, Mac," while peeling the plastic wrapper from the pack.

"Sure thing," I say, right before I happen to notice the day's date on one of the papers.

"Hey," I laugh, "it's my birthday!"

"Seriously?" Doyle says, "It's really your birthday today?"

"Yes," I reply, turning to face him with a smile.

"Then happy birthday," he says on handing me a cigarette. "How old are you," he jokes, "twenty-two?"

"Sure," I say with a grin, deciding not to tell him I'm seventeen for a reason I can't explain. I know he didn't believe me when I told him I was twenty-one but he's never asked me for the truth and if it doesn't bother him, why should I let it bother me?

"Happy twenty-second," he grins and he lights his cigarette before bringing the flame of his lighter closer to me. Lighting my cigarette, I can't help but notice the faint scar on one of his knuckles, the scar he got on the night he came to my rescue and pulled the intruder from me. It's funny; although that happened a fairly long time ago, I'll sometimes panic if we're walking the streets and I hear somebody come running up from behind. And in LA, you nearly always have some fitness freak running by.

"Thanks," I say once my cigarette is burning. It's a hot day so the smoke feels a little too heavy but I didn't want to decline Doyle's offer of a cigarette and look rude because of it.

"You know what we should do?" he asks once we're walking again. "We should get some liquor in tonight and celebrate."

"Where're we going to get that?"

"A few people will happily hand over a bottle they happen to have if we tell them it's your birthday," he says, and I believe him because I know a lot of people really like him. "If we need any more," he adds with a shrug, "we'll lift it from the stores."

"Thanks," I say, "I mean that."

"Forget about it," he shrugs. All of a sudden, a black limousine with darkened windows is crawling along beside us. I think I hear Doyle release a sigh but he carries on walking, looking straight ahead like he wants to pretend he hasn't noticed the car. Me, I can't help but admiringly look at it. It's a beautiful car and it clearly wasn't cheap.

The car continues to follow us until one of the windows near the back eases down to reveal a chubby-faced man wearing horn-rimmed spectacles. The heat has made his skin puffy and pink and a layer of perspiration has set up base just beneath his hairline. "Doyle," the man says before speaking up a little louder. "Father Doyle," he says.

I turn to Doyle and, filled with wonder, I ask him, "What is this?"

"Don't worry about it," he says to me before turning to the chubby man like he's only just heard him or noticed the limo. "Mark," he confidently says, taking his first steps to the vehicle which comes to an immediate halt now they- whoever *they* are- have Doyle's attention. "Mark Chambers."

Chambers thrusts a hand out for Doyle to take, and he does. The two men shake hands and people on the street look to us as discreetly as they can manage, hoping to see a major movie star like Tom Cruise or maybe even Harrison Ford. I notice as Doyle brings his hand back, he quickly wipes it against the side of his leg. Maybe the chubby man he knows as Mark Chambers has hands as sweaty as his face, maybe his touch just leaves you feeling dirty. "That's right," Chambers nods, "that's right." He tosses me the quickest of glances before putting his eyes back on Doyle. "So," he says with a nod and a polite smile that shows his ridiculously whitened teeth, "what have you been up to?"

"You know me," Doyle says, "spreading the word of God, loving my fellow man. If it's good, I've been doing it."

"Wonderful," Chambers says. "So where is it you two are headed?" he asks but before Doyle even has the chance to answer Chambers throws a second question at him. "Who is your friend, anyway?"

Doyle throws a glance back at me like he'd forgotten I'm with him. "This is Lee," he says. "He's family."

"How nice," Chambers says despite how obvious it is to see he knows that was a lie.

"Listen," he says, "we're just off to get some lunch and it would be great if you and *Lee* were to come with us. It's been far too long and it would be great to catch-up with you."

"I'm sorry," Doyle says, "but we'll have to take a rain check. We've got to be at-"

"We'll drop you off after lunch," Chambers says, "or before, if that's more convenient?"

"I don't want to impose," Doyle says.

"Father Doyle," Chambers says as the driver climbs out of the front (dressed just like you expect them to be; smart suit, black sunglasses, cap with visor and a haircut you could set your watch to) so he can open the door Chambers is sitting beside, "*we* can't just let you and your family member go on without having a nice meal with us first."

"Well," Doyle says back to me with a sigh as the driver reaches out for the door handle, "I guess an hour or two won't put us out by too much, right?"

23

It's funny, following Doyle into the back of a limo... Funny because we have to keep our toothbrushes (and tube of toothpaste) in a refrigerator so mice or rats won't be able to chew on them. Funny because I'd never have guessed he knows people who have a chauffeur-driven limousine taking them around the finer parts of LA. But following Doyle into the back of a limousine with an air conditioner working to keep us cool despite the heat, I try not to laugh with excitement on finding myself on a long leather chair as the driver gently closes the door after me.

Chambers isn't the only person sitting in the back. There's a girl of around thirty, sexy in a geeky way because of her spectacles and drab clothing with 'safe' haircut- sitting with a large handbag on her lap and just to the side of her is a woman I recognise from my youth. I didn't know her personally or anything, it's just she was one of the big stars in a daytime drama that mom used to watch when I was young. I smile in her direction because she's famous (only a couple of small film roles to her name but she still gets a lot of parts on big TV shows) but for the life of me, I can't recall her name or make sense of her appearance. Her skin is too smooth due to cosmetic surgery and her eyes are too pinched for the same reason. Maybe that's why the black beret she's wearing has a veil of black lace hanging over her eyes, I don't know. She's wearing a cream jacket over her green summer dress. The summer dress draws attention to her tits. They're too perky; too high and tight for a woman of her age so again, I think of surgical enhancements.

She acts like she's yet to notice me and brings the long cigarette she is holding to her plump lips. "Doyle," she says with a grin, "I knew it was you the minute I saw you walking out of that rundown store."

He smiles back at her. "Tiffany," he says, "you look as lovely as always," and her name comes flooding back to me. Tiffany Lily. She played Holly Keating in the show my mom used to watch.

"And you," she purrs. "You remember Mark, don't you? Still my agent," she says before laughing, "but for the life of me, I don't know why! And this," she adds, holding an open hand out in front of the girl beside her, "is Samantha. Samantha is my new personal assistant. Couldn't live without you, could I?" she asks Samantha, causing the young girl to blush.

"It's such a surprise," Tiffany says, "seeing you like this. I was only thinking about you recently, at a ceremony I attended. Awards of some kind," she continues like she's already bored of talking about it, "you know how it is, you know somebody involved and they ask you to go so it gets a little extra press? I still don't know who half of the winners were, but there were quite a few familiar faces. Jagger was there making a big deal about some member of England's royal family he had over at a party or something and a number of other musicians. Actors, too," she adds. "Roger Moore," she smiles, "still posing with that signature eyebrow of his. I was almost a Bond girl," she says. "Did I ever tell you that?"

"Yes," Doyle says, hand delving into a pocket for the cigarettes and lighter within. I follow suit, certain I should have a few cigarettes remaining but I'm just as sure that I've left the Zippo back in my room. "You've mentioned it once before."

"I couldn't do it," she explains before pausing just long enough to blow smoke at the ceiling, "due to another project. But I'm glad I couldn't," she shrugs, "because Bond girls tend to disappear. I can't even remember the name of the girl who took the part in the end. Mark," she asks her agent, "who took the part in the end?"

"I don't know," he admits, "I wasn't your agent at the time."

"Then find out," she says before turning to face her young PA, Samantha. "Call the restaurant," she says. "Tell them I'm going to need two more chairs."

Samantha nods and reaches for the telephone I hadn't noticed until now. I'm sitting in the back of a limousine that has its own telephone sitting right across from an incredibly wealthy actress.

"There was one person who really stood out at the party," she tells Doyle, "which is pretty ironic, seeing that he'll be forgotten about in no time at all. Tell me," she asks, "have you ever heard of Tony Warr? He's the singer of a rock n roll band."

"I've seen him in one or two magazines," he replies, "but I couldn't name any of his songs."

"No," she says, "I don't think anybody here could. But anyway he was at the party, wearing a torn prom-dress and smudged makeup with fake blood and cuts all over him. You know what he said when Bette asked him *why* he had come as a prom-night-zombie? He said he wasn't a prom-night zombie but a young girl who had been brutally raped by the 'jock' she attended the prom with. Really," she asks, "is that what we are supposed to class as intelligent entertainment?"

Tiffany doesn't want an answer so she doesn't allow Doyle to offer one. Instead she looks to me for the first time as she asks him, "So this is a relative of yours?"

"Sure," Doyle nods as transparent blue smoke flows out from his mouth. "This is my cousin, Lee."

"*Lee*," the TV star says right back at me with a warm smile and it's almost impossible for me not to laugh out with nerves or excitement. I can't help but wonder how mom would have reacted knowing I would one day sit in the back of a limousine with Holly Keating herself (although I do make a mental note of *not* calling her that to her face). "And where are you from, Lee?"

"Texas," Doyle answers for me and his answer has me taken aback. His answer has me wondering if I should maybe put on a Texan accent, but I'm not completely sure to how they sound so I decide it's for the best that I don't.

"Texas," Tiffany says back to me, sounding real impressed, "just like our latest president. It's funny how I've always wanted to go to Texas but I've never had a good enough reason so I've never found the time regardless of how many times George's people invite me. Where about in Texas are you from?"

"Houston," I blurt out. To try and make it sound that little bit more believable I add, "You know, Houston, like the singer?"

"Of course," Tiffany says, smiling real wide because I've

brought a famous singer into the conversation. "It's funny," she says, "isn't it… Houston's association with NASA and then a star on earth shares the name!"

Doyle chuckles so I follow his lead and laugh along with him. I notice for the first time how Samantha is no longer talking on the telephone but rummaging through her handbag. Tiffany's agent, the hot and sweaty Mark Chambers is playing around with a toothpick with his eyes right on Doyle as he smiles nervously, nods his head and laughs from time to time but it's clear to see he's feeling uncomfortable. Lucky for him, I'm the only one paying him the slightest nod of attention and my thoughts clearly mean shit to him.

"In case you haven't already guessed," Doyle says to me, "Miss Lily here knows a lot of influential people."

"Please," she says to me with another warm smile, "call me Tiffany. But anyway," she asks, "*Lee*, have you followed your cousin into doing God's work?"

"I don't know," I say, a little embarrassed to be put on the spot like this. Even Chambers is looking right at me now, so I can't look at his own sense of unease to make myself feel better. "What I mean is," I try desperately to explain, "don't we all follow God's will in our own way? Like you," I add, "you have this remarkable, God-given talent, and you just *knew* you had to share it with the world. You just *knew*," I finish.

For a moment that stretches out for a lifetime, everybody in the car simply looks at me and I can't help but wonder if I took it a little too far. But eventually, Tiffany smiles and says, "I couldn't have put it better myself." She looks to Doyle and carries on smiling, like the skin of her face has been stretched far too tight and now it's a great effort to change expression. "It looks like you aren't the only charming member of the Doyle family."

Relieved, I finally get around to lighting my cigarette and slump back in the incredibly comfortable seat I've somehow found myself in. All too happy to let Doyle handle things from here, I pretend to be looking out of the window and resist the urge to mention just how smoothly the car is moving along. A blanket of ice is bumpier.

"Now, now," Doyle says, "you know better than to use that silver tongue of yours on a man of God."

"Please," Tiffany says, and she surprises me by leaning forward as if to look Doyle square in the eye as she continues but she drops a hand on my knee and gives it a squeeze, "Bill is the only person you can truly describe as having a silver tongue! He invited me to a party just last week," she says pulling her hand away and leaning back in her seat, leaving me to wonder if anybody else noticed how she had grabbed me… whether it was a mistake, maybe and she had been meaning to take a hold of Doyle's knee but found mine instead. "Not just me," she gushes, "and not just him," she laughs. "Hillary would have been there… Or so he wanted me to believe!"

"You have to watch yourself around this one," Doyle says bringing his elbow into my side. "She's quick-witted and could make it clear for all to see if she made a circus clown blush."

"What can I say?" she grins, stubbing out her cigarette and immediately snatching the handbag from Samantha so her slender hands can search within for another, "I've attended Hugh's pool parties, dined with Warren in the finest restaurants Europe has to offer and danced with Jack in the most exclusive of clubs. Not one of these men had to seek votes for their power," she adds with an arched brow, "or their attraction. Men in office," she assures me, "always need us a lot more than we need them."

"Tiffany," Chambers desperately informs me, "did *not* just say that."

"Yes I did," she winks. "And I'll tell you something, not one of those men knows how to tip."

24

THE DRIVER OPENS the door for us and I climb out of the back right after Doyle, who himself followed Chambers who followed Samantha. Tiffany comes out last, taking her time so the onlookers will be able to accept it's really her. The restaurant we've arrived at is called KNEWMAN'S and as Tiffany links her arm through mine she whispers, "The *K* is silent," into my ear. "Thanks for letting me know," I say only because I can't think of anything else. But we all head inside the place and Chambers marches right over to a guy standing behind a podium with an open book on it and he says something real fast and real quiet. The man nods in understanding, greets us all but none more so than Tiffany and then he leads us through the restaurant with promises to Tiffany about how we'll be seated in a real private spot. Of course, reaching this destination requires us to walk by every other diner and some of them- I'm guessing out-of-luck-writers desperate to pass a screenplay on to somebody or bit-part actors hoping to meet the 'right' person- look over at us with open mouths but don't dare approach. Tiffany is clearly loving the attention but she's making out like she hasn't noticed it. Personally, I think most of the looks are made because a man of the church unexpectedly happens to be a member of her entourage. Maybe they're even wondering who that particularly hot stud at her side is?

"Have you ever dined here before?" she asks me in a hushed whisper.

"Only the once," I lie and luckily, before she can ask me for any extra details, the man we're following takes us to a hidden corner of the room where a table for five is waiting. It takes me all of two seconds to realise we'll have to walk by everybody else again if we need to visit the bathroom.

"Your table," the man proudly says to Tiffany. Chambers, Samantha and even Doyle pick a chair. The waiter goes to

83

ease one out from under the table but Tiffany stops him from completing his job by saying, "Don't do that, Lee here is a gentleman," she claims, removing her hand from my arm so she can stand beside the chair, waiting for me to seat her.

"Of course," he says and everybody looks at me. Feeling a little nervous, feeling like I'll somehow manage to get *moving a chair* wrong. I take hold of the back and ease it out just enough for Tiffany to be seated.

"Thank you," she says and I tell her it wasn't a problem before realising how the only available seat is the one beside her, like everybody else in the group conspired against me. I smile, sigh a little out of nerves and take the seat. The waiter nods at me with a grin, glad he can finally get to work. "Could I recommend-" he begins.

"There aren't any flowers," Tiffany says loud enough for us all to hear. "No flowers, no menus. It's like we didn't even tell them we were coming here today."

"There are no flowers," Chambers says to the guide that brought us here. "Every other table we went by had flowers but ours doesn't? And no menus?" He says, "How're we meant to know what we want to eat?"

"I'm sorry, but we had to bring in a larger table once we realised there would be five of you and not three; somebody must have forgotten to place the flowers and menus on *this* table during the resetting."

"Is that supposed to be an excuse?" Chambers laughs in disbelief and looks to each of us in turn as he asks, "What's supposed to be happening here, are we just supposed to know what's on the menu or something? Maybe smell the waiter's cologne in place of flowers?"

"Mark," Tiffany says like she's bored already, "leave the poor man alone, we did play a part in this with changing our plans so unexpectedly. Five menus," she smiles at the waiter, "and a bottle of wine with five glasses. Somebody here will know what I like."

"Of course," the waiter says, "I'll get them right away," he assures us on leaving.

"Father Doyle," Tiffany asks with a smile, "how long has it been?"

"A year," he says, "maybe even two?"

"Where does the time go?" she wants to know.

Doyle just smiles at her and shrugs his shoulders. I get the impression he's feeling a little uncomfortable by the way he's fidgeting... the way he takes a cigarette from his pack and taps it twice against the table, lifting it to his mouth but stopping his hand halfway. "Are we even allowed to smoke in here?" he asks.

"You're with me," Tiffany proudly claims, "you can do whatever you want right now." I'm already growing tired of her attitude. It's not like she's set Hollywood alight with her talents.

"What can I say?" Doyle smirks as he takes his lighter from his pocket, "I can't keep up with all these *No Smoking* laws that are flying around the country." He lights his cigarette, takes a quick pull on it and exhales before looking at me like he's only just remembered I'm here. "You want a cigarette?"

"I've got some," I say taking a hold of my pack, "but I'd appreciate a light. I can't find mine," I say patting down my pockets.

"Probably dropped it in the car," he says, sliding his lighter across the table and into my hands. I'm lighting my cigarette when Tiffany drops a well-manicured hand on my lap and asks, "Could you give me one of your cigarettes, Lee?"

"Sure," I say handing her a smoke. She waits for me to hold a light out for her so that is what I do. The waiter returns, pauses for a moment as he takes a look at who's smoking and who isn't, but hands out the menus without saying a single word as another suddenly appears and places a vase filled with blooming roses down on the table. A third is right behind them both with a bottle of wine and five glasses.

<h1 style="text-align:center">25</h1>

THE WHITE WINE Tiffany prefers tastes just like any other white wine to me, like shit. As far as I'm concerned, white wine tastes like white wine and red wine tastes like red wine. People can spend a fortune on it but I've never tasted any real difference yet between a cheap bottle and a reasonably expensive bottle. Noticing the involuntary shudder I give after each swallow, Tiffany places her hand atop of mine and smiles. "Not to your liking?" she asks.

"It's nothing personal," I assure her, "it's just all wine tastes the same to me."

"Ha!" she says to Chambers or Samantha. "Uncultured pallet. Don't worry," she says turning back to me as she pats my hand, "I'll have you educated yet."

"Just like My Fair Lady," Chambers offers with a smile but both go unnoticed as far as Tiffany is concerned. Her eyes have fallen back onto Doyle.

"I can't believe how long it's been. How long has it been since we last saw each other?" she asks for the third or fourth time.

"Around two years," he says.

"Two years," she repeats back to him. "Are you still living in that old tenement building on Grove Street?"

"No," Doyle says, shaking his head. "I've been out of there for quite a while."

"With a new friend," Tiffany says, "how exciting! So where exactly are you staying these days?" she asks him. Doyle grins at her and simply says, "Around."

"Men of mystery," Tiffany laughs softly. "How did I keep myself entertained without you?"

Deciding what everybody is to drink isn't enough for the big star and she has to decide what we all eat. I usually wouldn't complain, a free meal and free drinks are exactly that, but it's just the way she does it to remind us all how she is in charge.

She even leaves a little food on her own plate but will pick some from Samantha's despite the fact they are enjoying the same meal.

Chambers' cellphone starts ringing all of a sudden. He takes it from his pocket, examines the caller ID and immediately answers it with, "Chambers. Uh-huh," he nods, *"uh-huh..."* he adds, momentarily oblivious to the angry look Tiffany has tossed in his direction. He finally notices it, mouths an apology to his client and says, "just give me one minute, would you?" down the line as he rises from his chair and leaves the table to continue his conversation elsewhere.

"I hate those things," Tiffany says a second before adding, "and cellphones are almost as bad!" with a laugh. Samantha smiles politely to her boss before looking back down at her plate so she can pick away at the food, careful not to take too much in case Tiffany is still a little hungry.

"That was delicious," Doyle says, pushing his plate into the heart of the table. I realise he hasn't eaten much and that confuses me. I mean, we mostly live on breakfast cereal, cookies and fruit. Here we are at a fine restaurant that doesn't put much on your plate as it is but will happily charge you a fortune and he's making out he can't eat all of it? "But Tiffany," he says lighting another cigarette, "how're things in the industry? Are you working at the minute?"

She carries on smiling at him but I notice a look of anger in her eyes for just a second. "Of course," she tells him, "of course. I've been asked to audition for a few movie roles but I don't know if the parts are for me. And I'm still on television throughout most of the year."

"Television," he says, "that's good. One-off appearances or continuing roles?"

"A mixture," she says, still smiling. "Everything is changing so much," she explains. "Nobody wants a mature drama anymore; they want soap operas for teenagers with stories about drink driving or underage pregnancies. And don't get me started on this whole *Reality TV* explosion."

"Drink driving and underage pregnancies," Doyle says,

leaning back in his chair and shaking his head like he missed the last part entirely. "And you do know half the people playing teenagers are pushing thirty, don't you? Still," he adds before Tiffany can answer him, "at least you're still getting work. What roles do they tend to be," he asks, "parent or aunt?"

Tiffany smiles at Doyle but she doesn't answer him. She turns to me instead and asks, "What about you, Lee, do you watch any television when you're not with your cousin here?" I try to remember whether we had said we're cousins or something else… Try to decide whether I should correct her or not but no words come from my mouth. All of this unexpectedness and the lies are becoming too much for me to keep track of.

"Tiffany, please," Doyle says to her, "Lee is from Texas. All he ever wants to watch is the football."

"Of course," she says to me, "I'd forgotten you're from Texas. You must be proud of George W. right now, mustn't you? Sitting in the oval office but still finding time to work back at the ranch. I met him at a party a number of years ago," she claims. "This was when he was a little too dependent on alcohol, of course. Oh," she says, "how George and Barbara used to worry about him. Still, it all turned out right in the end, didn't it?"

"Not really," Doyle says, looking off to the side as he brings his cigarette to his mouth. "The man became president. Twice" he adds with a smirk.

"He's doing what he thinks is best for the country," Tiffany claims. "Still," she says, "you know what is going to happen at the next presidential election, don't you? We'll have a Clinton back in the White House. First female president; mark my words."

26

"I wish you wouldn't try and be so damned mysterious," Tiffany says to Doyle. "I can have the driver drop you off right at your door… assuming you have one of those."

We're all back in the black limousine. We've all finished our meals, our glasses of wine and the obligatory coffee that follows dessert. Tiffany goes from acting like I'm the only person she's with to grilling Doyle on where we're staying, where the driver should drop us off, how people are expected to get in touch with us in case of an emergency. And Doyle just keeps batting her away. He's even told her to drop us off at Grove Street despite her already knowing we don't live there and despite my not having a clue where Grove Street is. But the driver is taking us there anyway and I really wish he wasn't.

All I can see on the other side of the limousine windows are abandoned factories and boarded up buildings. Whenever we have to stop at a red light, hookers or crack dealers on the corners perk up and wait for somebody to wind a window down a little to call them over but nobody does and I'm glad. I'm glad every time the lights turn to amber and we can get moving again because I'm scared that eventually, one of those dealers won't be happy at just staring in our direction.

"Tiffany," Doyle says, smiling as he takes a leisurely pull on his cigarette, "your problems are all down to how you've surrounded yourself with people that do what you say, when you say it. You should be thanking me for showing you how you can't always get what you want."

Doyle is enjoying this a lot more than he's letting on, I can tell and I'm sure Tiffany can. Chambers is talking to somebody on his cellphone, or pretending to so he doesn't have to get involved and Samantha is marking something down in a book she pulled from her leather handbag as she speaks to somebody on the telephone. Clearly annoyed, Tiffany turns to me and asks, "Are you sure you two are related? He doesn't have you manners or your looks. Could there have been a mix up of some sort at the hospital?"

"This'll do," Doyle suddenly announces catching sight, or at least pretending to, of something on the street outside. He raps his knuckles against the partition glass between us and the driver and says, "Pull over, would you?"

"Give me strength," Tiffany says and she lifts what looks to be another telephone from her side of the vehicle. "Stop once you get the chance," she says, "and don't worry about opening the door." She places the receiver back down and shakes her head at Doyle like he's a child who has just been caught misbehaving. "If drivers heard half the things that are said in the back of a limo," she tells him, "they would be able to buy their own tropical islands with the money they made selling exclusives to the press."

The limo pulls up at the kerb. Doyle smiles to Tiffany. "Thank you for a wonderful evening," he says, "but this is mine and Lee's stop. But this was fun," he adds opening the car door, "we should really do this again sometime."

Tiffany snaps her fingers. Hearing the signal, Samantha quickly reaches into the handbag and unearths a card she slips into the star's hand. "It was a pleasure to make your acquaintance," Tiffany says holding the card out for me to take. "Let me know if you'd ever like to see the parts of LA that your cousin can't get into."

Doyle is already standing on the sidewalk. Not wanting to hurt Tiffany's feelings, I take the card and slip it into my back pocket. "Thanks," I say, "for the meal and everything. It was real considerate of you. Kind, even."

"Only money," she smiles back at me. "Don't be a stranger. And feel free to bring Doyle along, I'm sure I can find something to keep him entertained. A colouring-in book, maybe."

"Okay," I say and I step out of the vehicle and turn to say goodbye but Chambers pulls the door shut as soon as he can and the black limousine is moving on again without as much as a single wave.

"Well," I say to Doyle, "that was new." He reaches for his cigarettes, extracts one and leaves me wondering why he isn't offering me a smoke. Wondering if I've somehow offended him, I scan my immediate surroundings as he lights up. Wherever we are, whether this is actually Grove Street or just someplace close to it, it looks like shit. There are no cars on the road and I'm glad there isn't, because this looks like the kind of place where drive-bys happen from time to time.

"It gets real old," Doyle finally says, "real fast. Come on, let's walk home."

Keeping at his side, I remain silent until it's clear to see he's not going to say anything else so I do. "I used to watch a show she was on back when I was a little boy. My mom loved it," I say with a smile, hoping that revealing something about my past will encourage him to ask me a question or two.

"Yeah," Doyle says, pausing as smoke drifts out from between his teeth real slow, "she used to be pretty famous some ten or so years back."

"How do you know her, anyway?"

Doyle opens his mouth to answer but decides against it. Whatever he had been about to say, you know it falls away with the shaking of his head. "My problem with people like her," he finally says, "and not just Tiffany Lily but actors in general-"

I can't help but interrupt him. "Isn't she an actress?" I ask. "You know, men are actors, women are actresses."

"Whatever," he shrugs. "The streets here are crawling with them. And my problem with them - with *all* of them - is you can never know them... not really. They're always playing at being something else, somebody else, for what's happening around them at that particular moment. You can't trust them when they're trying to make it," he says, "and you sure as hell can't trust them once they have made it. You saw her with those two people she has, just to hang on to her every word, to tell her how great she is. She collects people like that and if you're not careful," he warns, "she'll take to collecting people like you."

I open my mouth to speak but can't think of anything else to say, so we just walk on for a while in silence. "Look at that,"

I finally say pointing to something discarded on the sidewalk "That used condom looks a lot like an elephant's trunk left on the sidewalk."

27

WE'RE STILL WALKING along what may or may not be Grove Street and if I ever thought the area that we live in now is a slum, I take it all back. I'm scared I'll step on the chalk outline of a murder victim if I don't keep my eyes peeled. "So you really used to live here?" I ask.

"For a while," Doyle nods. "It's not as bad as it looks once you know a few of the local residents."

"Why did you leave?"

Doyle shrugs. "I can't say I formed any kind of emotional attachment to the place," he says, "and something better revealed itself to me so I never came back one day."

We pass a broken, defeated black man sitting in the mouth of an alleyway. Head bowed, he has his back pressed against the wall. He's wearing a filthy military jacket of some sort with beige jeans and shoes that are being kept together by sticky-tape. "Spare change?" he asks as we pass. "Sorry," Doyle says and we keep on walking.

"Are there any good bars around here?" I ask, hoping to remind Doyle how it's my birthday and his promise to provide some alcohol for it. I realise I'm in the act of lighting a cigarette, like I'm real nervous he'll let my birthday pass by without celebrating it first and my hunch that he's pissed at me will be proven right.

"There used to be," Doyle says. "I can't promise they'll still be a place to go without getting into any trouble, but we can have a look either way."

Hearing fast, clumsy footsteps coming up from behind us, we both look back to see it's the black man in the army jacket. I make fists in case he attacks either of us but I'm also hoping he doesn't see my fists as cause to attack. The man slows down nearing us and grins. His teeth are discoloured and chipped. One at the front looks to be covered in mould. "Doyle! I knew it was you," he says, "I *knew* it was you!"

Doyle leans back an inch and gets a real good look at the man. "Owen?" Doyle grins. "Jesus Christ," he says, "is that you, Owen?"

"The one and only!" the black guy laughs. Doyle takes to laughing alongside him and the two embrace right there on the street. I'm wondering who Owen is exactly but even more than that, I'm hoping to God he won't come back to Saint Claire's with us.

28

SITTING ON A park bench with Owen, I wonder how much longer Doyle is going to be and I wonder if he's gone off alone to get some drinks, leaving me here with somebody I have never even seen before, just to get back at me. But get back at me for what, being polite to Tiffany Lily? I followed *him* into the limousine. She stopped after seeing *him*, not me.

Once more, Owen tells me how relieved he is to see Doyle again. "Didn't have a clue what happened to him for all these years. Heck," he grins, "I still don't! Remind me to ask him when he gets back, would you?"

Once more, he asks me how it is I know Doyle and how long I've been hanging with him. Asks me where it is we're staying exactly and playing it safe, I claim it depends on where we're close to. Owen doesn't smell too bad apart from when he opens his mouth to talk- which is a lot. More than anything, I want a cigarette but I resist the urge because it would mean offering him one and that responsibility should be on Doyle, not me.

And at long last, Doyle comes walking towards us. He's carrying a six-pack of Heineken and I can't help but wonder how he got those out of the door without a shopkeeper noticing him, especially if he didn't have me there to cause a distraction. Could Doyle have had a little extra money in his pocket? Money he didn't want me to know about? I try not to spend too long thinking about it. With a little luck, the walk to the store will have been enough to clear his mind and have him drop whatever problem he clearly has with me all of a sudden.

Owen only has eyes for Doyle now and as our mutual friend draws ever nearer I see how he's smoking a cigarette and light one of my own now his friend isn't paying me any attention. "Sure is a hot night," Doyle remarks. Owen moves up a little closer to me, giving Doyle a little space so he can join us on the bench. Doyle thanks him, sits down and takes to tearing the cardboard that keeps the bottles together in half. I'll be honest, a part of me is expecting him to take one bottle for himself and one for Owen before leaving me high and dry but he hands one to Owen and Owen immediately passes it to me. "Thanks," I say taking the cap off. The bottle is surprisingly cold, like it's fresh from the refrigerator and I thank God for that because the humidity in the air is pressing its full weight down on me, letting me know how LA is soon to be engulfed by a terrible heat that will torment me until a thunderstorm finally arrives to bring it all to an end.

"To old friends," Doyle says raising his drink, letting me know without shadow of a doubt he has his panties in a bunch about something I've done and the planned celebration regarding my birthday has been tossed to the wind.

"And new ones," Owen adds.

"Old friends," I reluctantly sigh on bringing the cold bottle to my lips.

"Man," Owen tells Doyle, "I was just saying to Lee how good it is to see you. Good, and sure unexpected! I asked a lot of people about you," he says, "about your whereabouts, and nobody had any idea about either. Some thought you'd become another John Doe that the cops had to fish out of the docks, others were sure you were in prison. Hell," he grins, "I was sure it was the latter!"

"Not a prison that can hold me," Doyle claims. "If they threw me back inside, I'd kill myself just to get out of there."

Owen laughs long and hard at that last comment, whereas I simply pay attention. In all the months I've been with Doyle, we've never once talked about prison. I've never been inside and I guess I just assumed he was the same. The off-white dog collar around his neck leads you to believe he could get away with anything.

Doyle smirks, shakes his head from side to side and takes a slow drag on his cigarette before he talks again. "I'm deadly serious," he says. "Anything longer than six months and I'd be coming out in a box after a matter of days."

"You know what that means, don't you?" Owen sniggers.

Doyle smirks at him and asks, "What?"

Owen shakes his head from side to side this time and laughs again. "They could arrest you for stealing a pack of chewing gum and you'd be looking at more than six months, given your history!"

"Then it'd never make it to court," Doyle says with a shrug. "They'd never grant me bail," he sighs, "and I couldn't afford it anyway if they did, so they'd keep me locked up until the trial and I'd slip my head in a noose before it had a chance to begin."

All Doyle's talk about suicide and death... It's all brand new to me. I've never heard him talk this way before. If all conversations with Owen go something like this, I can understand why he left the area to settle down at Saint Claire's instead. The last thing you want or need when you're out on the streets is people only willing to make a bad situation worse.

"But what about you," Doyle says to Owen, "what's new with you?"

"Death sentence of my own," Owen says, still smiling as he lifts the bottle to his lips.

"Don't be cryptic," Doyle smirks, "fill me in already."

"AIDS," Owen reveals and I find myself edging away from him by a couple of millimetres.

"Fuck," Doyle says, "please tell me you're only yanking my chain."

"Be a pretty sick motherfucker if that was my sense of humour," Owen smiles at him. "Full-blown AIDS," he says. "It can't be that bad though, right? I mean, come winter, I get a cold, I die of pneumonia! A whole lot of worrying will come to an end on my half that way. Best of all, I'll probably go in a warm hospital bed with a full stomach and a lot of good morphine inside of me!"

"But I just don't get it." Doyle asks, "Why are you still on the streets? There's got to be a hostel that would take you in given your... current condition."

"*Current condition*," Owen laughs, "because my *next condition* is going to be *dead*! Boy," he says, "I sure did miss you and your way with words."

"I'm being serious here," Doyle says, "why're you still out on the streets?"

"Why're any of us?" Owen shrugs his shoulders. "There are hostels, charities, all kinds of places willing to take us in and try and put our lives in order," he says and I bite my tongue instead of suggesting he never try the church. "But they all have that one rule," he smirks, "that one rule that keeps us all from the door."

"What is it?" I ask.

"Don't you know?" he asks, turning to face me with a grin that forces me to stare at his rotten teeth closer than ever. "They say you're not allowed to drink on the premises... Not even allowed on the premises if you smell of beer. They're even harder on drugs. They'll pat your pockets down and if you're carrying pills without a doctor's note alongside them, you either hand them over to be flushed or you walk."

"People tend to walk," Doyle says on flicking cold ash from the end of his cigarette. "Who'd want to give their hard-earned gains over for some college student or nun to pocket once they're in the bathroom?"

"Exactly!" Owen laughs, "Exactly! You just know they're taking whatever they get their greedy hands on as payment. Fuck," he says, "if I was surrounded by winos and drop-outs, I'd be taking Prozac like you would never believe!"

"That's too bad," Doyle jokes, "you're being surrounded by winos and drop-outs right now, and they say you're not supposed to mix Prozac with alcohol."

"Same with Valium," Owen says, "but we all do." He downs the contents of his bottle and tosses it aside so it shatters on the floor. "Speaking of such, do you have any on you?"

Doyle asks him, "Any what?"

"Prozac," he says, "Valium."

And I know we have a little Valium back at Saint Claire's. But I don't know if Doyle will suggest we all go back there to do it or if this was Owen's plan to get a roof over his head all along.

"Not on me," Doyle says, shaking his head again whilst guiding his beer to his lips.

"Well isn't this your lucky day?" Owen says, "You just happen to bump into an old friend who lives nearby and has recently got plenty of those little treats given over to him! You're both welcome to come back with me, free room, free mood lighteners..."

Doyle laughs.

"What do you say?" Owen asks, "What do you both say?"

I say, "I'm in."

29

Waking with a throbbing headache, I open my eyes and the sight of squalor that greets me only makes me wish I hadn't. The room we followed Owen back to is horrific at best; the plaster on the walls has fallen off in chunks, allowing wooden bars that make me think of an exposed ribcage to be seen. The plaster that hasn't fallen to the ground is covered in gang-tags. Pizza boxes and pages torn from old newspapers and magazines cover the floor, as do empty bottles of alcohol and crushed cans of beer. I spot a couple of empty wine bottles and remember the needless risks Doyle took to get them a couple of hours earlier. With a hand at my temple I groan, sitting up. Just beyond my feet and pressed against the wall, Owen sleeps soundly. Looking behind me, I see Doyle flat on his back with his mouth open and his eyes closed. The butt of a cigarette that must have burned out as he was falling asleep is still between two of his fingers.

I pull myself up onto shaky legs and stretch. Looking at the floor, I can't help but wonder where it is exactly all the cigarette ends disappear to. There are a couple of rat traps here and there but they're all missing bait. I go to smoke a cigarette but stop learning I only have the one left, so it would be a good idea to save it. I take a step closer to Doyle but decide against waking him when I remember how off he was with me last night. I take a deep breath to clear my head, take one last look at the room and head for the door that isn't attached at the hinges but has been pressed into the doorjamb. Moving it aside, I step out onto the small hallway and make my way downstairs.

There's a smell of piss and damp all around me. Offensive slogans have been sprayed onto the tight walls. Pornographic magazines have been torn to shreds and discarded on the steps. Some of the pages are crinkled where *something* has soaked into them. Reaching the front door which is heavy and holding at least six locks, all broken during the last police raid. I ease it open and step out onto the street. The morning sun hurts my eyes. Cars go by on the road, an endless flow of traffic and exhaust fumes. A shopping cart has been abandoned, turned upside down beside the stoop.

Scratching the back of my neck, I start walking without any idea where it is I'm headed. I've a feeling similar to the one that plagued me on my first few days of being in LA, a feeling caused by having no idea where I am mixed with the acceptance I have of knowing not one single soul here.

But I remind myself how this isn't my first day here and I *do* know people now...

I stop dead in my tracks and reach into my back pocket. The card Samantha handed over to me in the back of the limousine is there, right where I left it. Examining it, I see how it possesses nothing more than a single telephone number. Front and back, there isn't a single letter of the alphabet made available. But I already have the name I need to know. Smiling, I make my way to the first payphone I see and open the batwing doors like a gunslinger entering a saloon way out in the Wild West. A cigarette to calm my nerves would be great around now but I decide it's best to wait, just in case I get no answer. Sighing, I reach out for the telephone receiver and realise that there isn't one.

"Motherfucker," I mutter, shaking my head as I step out of the payphone box and walk on with hopes of finding another, and soon. For a while, I do wonder *why* somebody would make a payphone so worthless, especially in *this* neighbourhood. In a neighbourhood where most residents don't have a telephone to call their own, the payphones are the only thing they have to reach a dealer. Did an addict tear the receiver away after hearing how his dealer didn't have what he wanted, or are rival dealers committing such deeds to put a little pressure on the competition? Realising it's unlikely that I'll ever find an answer I give up thinking about it and keep on walking.

I'm already sticky with sweat come the time I find the next payphone. It's a hot day and my clothes are sticking to my skin because of it. My throat is as dry as chalk because I've had no luck finding a store that would be easy to steal from given the area I'm in and every cell of my body is screaming for nicotine.

I give a sigh of relief seeing how this payphone hasn't been pulled apart. Lifting the receiver, I dial the operator and request a reverse-charge call and hope I'm not pushing my luck here. I read out the number on the card, answer I'd like to talk with *Tiffany* and give *Cousin Lee* as my name. The line rings. I hope somebody answers soon because the glass walls of the payphone are only magnifying the rays of the sun. Noticing a discarded packet of Millbrook cigarettes at my feet, my heart leaps to the back of my throat in anticipation but when I open the pack there are no cigarettes left for me.

Los Angeles has no Patron Saint of Needy Smokers.

30

Sat high up the stone steps leading to the entrance of the public library, I'm sure the black limousine is the one I've been waiting so long for as soon as it parks at the bottom of them. I'm hoping more than anything that Tiffany Lily is in possession of a pack of cigarettes and maybe a bottle of chilled water as I approach the vehicle and reach out for the door handle. A feeling of panic claims me once the door doesn't open. It's locked, and I'm left wondering if maybe this *isn't* the limo I've been waiting for... Is the mayor sitting in the backseat, looking at me through the darkened glass and fearing for his life? But the driver climbs out and I recognise him as the same driver from yesterday. I give a slow sigh of relief and feel a lot of tension drop away from my muscles.

"Mr Lee," he says to me with a polite nod of the head accompanied by a politer smile as he heads to the door that refused to open for me.

"Hey," I smile back at him, "Mr...?"

"Larsen," he smiles on reaching for the handle. I wonder if I've gone and made his day simply by asking him his name.

"Thanks," I say as he pops the door open. I bend down low and climb into the back. Tiffany is sitting there, of course, and Samantha is placed beside her again. Samantha is, as is expected, speaking with somebody on the telephone while she makes notes in the book she carries around in the large handbag. The door gently closes shut behind me.

"Lee," Tiffany says with a proud smile, "it is a delight to hear from you again so soon! I like men who don't play games... I think I should tell you that right away."

"Thanks for coming to pick me up," I reply as the car starts moving.

"It wasn't a problem," she assures me. "Well," she asks, "where in the world is that bothersome cousin of yours?"

"Sleeping off a hangover," I tell her. "Do you have a spare cigarette?" Samantha lets go of the phone she's holding and keeps it balanced on her shoulder while also pressing her ear against it so she can reach inside the bag for some much-needed cigarettes.

"A hangover," Tiffany smirks. "You two were out celebrating something last night?"

"We were supposed to be but it didn't feel like it," I sigh as Samantha pulls a pack of cigarettes and a lighter from the bag before handing both over to Tiffany. Tiffany takes a cigarette, pops it into her mouth and lights it before handing the pack and lighter over to me. "Keep them," she insists and I offer no form of protest. "What were you celebrating," she asks, "or *supposed* to be celebrating?"

"My birthday," I say sucking smoke deep into my lungs. The cigarettes are Lights so you have to take longer drags on them but I slide them into my pocket anyway.

"Your birthday!" Tiffany excitedly repeats. "How old are you now?"

"Twenty-two," I lie.

"And the celebration didn't go as planned?"

"The celebration just didn't go," I smirk wiping beads of sweat from my forehead. I try not to picture the sweat patch I'll leave behind where I've been sitting. "We bumped into an old friend of Doyle's and he must have, well... clean forgot how it was my birthday."

"You don't have to lie to me," Tiffany smiles and she keeps her mouth closed just long enough for the smoke trail to finally leave her nostrils. "I know your cousin a lot better than anybody else does," she says. "For some strange reason, he had a problem with my buying you something to eat!"

"Yeah," I say, "you're probably right. You don't happen to have something cold I can drink, do you?"

Tiffany lifts the telephone receiver that has her able to talk with Larsen, the chauffeur. "Stop at the next store," she says, "and pick up a large bottle of-" she pauses as she raises her eyebrows to me.

"Anything," I shrug, a little embarrassed. "Dr Pepper," I say, "water, anything at all."

"Pick up a large bottle of Dr Pepper," she says, "and make sure it's cold, would you?" She places the receiver down and smiles at me. I smile back at her out of thanks. "So," she asks, "have you eaten today?"

"Not yet."

"Ha!" Tiffany says, "No offence, but that cousin of yours sure dropped the ball this year."

"Tell me about it," I smirk in a *what-can-you-do?* way.

"We're just heading back to my place," she says. "I can have something made for you, if you'd like? You can even have your clothes washed and dried while you take a shower or go for a dip in the pool."

"I wouldn't want to impose..."

"Nonsense," Tiffany says, pushing away my weighted concerns with a single wave of her hand. "Helping a Father's young cousin," she smirks, "is surely going to earn me a few karma points. Do you believe in karma," she asks, "or do you find that whole notion to be terribly blasphemous?"

"I don't know," I smile at her. "But if it helps people get along in life, I'm all for it."

31

LARSEN OPENS THE door and the sun that hits me is so bright I get an inkling to what dead souls witness when the gates of Heaven open up for them. Tiffany is the first to step out of the vehicle this time around and as she's telling me how her chef will be all too happy to make anything I like for me to eat, I glance over at Samantha to see if she's due out next but she moves her head ever so slightly to let me know it's me. I climb out of the vehicle, remember my bottle of Dr Pepper and turn to collect it but see Samantha is already carrying it out of the car for me. I thank her, turn back around and let my current surroundings wash over me for the first time. The limo has come to park in what I assume to be Tiffany's front yard, which is fucking huge to say the least. Sprinklers toss water over a well maintained lawn holding palm trees. A small white wall - easy enough to jump over - is all that stops the property from spilling out onto the street. The large houses opposite look just as nice but they're all white and combining that with the clear blue skies and high sun only has me feeling all the more uncomfortable

I turn and look to Tiffany's house, which is as white as the rest and just as big, if not a little larger. The term 'small mansion' comes to mind and I wonder if it's a real term or one I've just made up. With Tiffany, still talking nearing the front door, I make quick steps to catch up with her.

"I know it looks drab," she says, "but it really is the most convenient place for me to live when it comes down to work."

The large front door opens before she even places a manicured finger anywhere near the doorbell. A Spanish maid welcomes Tiffany into her own home and then smiles at me like we're already the best of friends. The home looks even bigger on the inside. Large, open archways open one room up to the next and natural light finds every corner of every room as overhead fans keep the temperature down low. Potted plants are so tall, so green and vibrant, that they come close to touching the ceiling. "How long have you lived here?" I ask.

"Eight years, maybe more," Tiffany says as she walks through the house with me following her like a loyal puppy. She leads me into a kitchen that is twice the size of my room at Saint Claire's, all marble and polished pine with the most modern of appliances. The entire back wall is glass; patio doors open to lead the way out onto the pool area. A guy of about my age or a little older is tanning himself on a sun lounger and wearing nothing but sunglasses and a pair of cream Speedos. A glass of orange juice rests on the floor beneath him. I open my mouth to ask Tiffany if that's her son but decide against it, just in case it's her lazy kid brother or something like Samantha's younger brother who gets all the benefits of knowing Tiffany without having to do any of the work. Tiffany turns to me and asks, "What would you like to eat?"

"I'm not hungry," I say, feeling a little embarrassed.

"Samantha," Tiffany says looking over my shoulder, "have somebody make Lee a sandwich. Lee," she says looking back at me, "come follow me, I have something to show you that I just *know* you're going to love."

I mouth a discreet apology to Samantha and follow Tiffany out of the kitchen and up to the next floor. The rooms have doors up here and framed movie posters decorate the walls. Tiffany is saying something about how she is planning to redecorate the place once she finds the time and then she leads me into a large room with a plush carpet on the floor and closed venetian blinds over the windows. A huge red leather couch is in front of a TV that takes up most of the wall. A bookcase holding video cassettes and DVDs stands at either side of the TV, audio speakers resting atop of them. "This," Tiffany smiles at me, "is the Media Room. It's really the heart of the house," she adds, stopping to take an open pack of cigarettes and a lighter from the arm of the couch. "Cigarette?" she asks. I accept her offer and we each light up.

"Every film I'm in," she says, "every TV show, the directors come to this room and we watch the first cut together and I let them know what I think. Too many people," she explains blowing smoke from her large lips, "are happy to just take the money and call it a day once they've finished their last scene. I stick with it to the very end."

"That's good," I say with a nod because I can't think of anything else to say to her. Still struggling I ask, "Are those *all* of the things you've ever appeared in?"

"Those?" she laughs looking back at the overcrowded bookcases. "My TV work alone would take up more than double that! No," she says, "I'm not one of those vain stars. I don't see the point in watching things I've appeared in over and over again. Some of those recordings," she continues, "are things I would like to see but haven't found the time, or they were made by somebody who has made things I've enjoyed before or they star people I admire or tried guiding at some point or another in their career. Name somebody," she challenges me, "and I'll let you know what they're really like."

"I don't know if I can," I chuckle.

"Nonsense," she smiles, lowering herself down onto the couch and patting the empty space beside her as she repositions herself so her feet are tucked under her tight ass. Obediently, I sit exactly where she has requested. "Come on," she says, "don't be shy. Consider it an exclusive."

"Okay," I laugh, and I think about my brother. I think about my brother and wonder if he's found his place in the world as easily as I have. I doubt he has and I'm a little glad about it giving the way he abandoned me, but I think about him anyway and I remember how his favourite movie of all time was *Blue Velvet* so I ask Tiffany, "What's David Lynch like?"

" David!" Tiffany laughs as she rolls her eyes. She takes a drag on her cigarette and I follow suit but I notice how there's already a build up of dead ash at the end of mine and I don't want it to drop onto the carpet and make a mess of the place. "David is..." she giggles, "David is *unique*. But he has a wonderful sense of humour and he's clearly very intelligent. Yes," she nods away, "I'd very much like to work with David in the near future. Name another," she says, "name anybody you can think of."

"Okay," I smile and, feeling a little bit more relaxed, I loosen up and try to think of a hot piece of ass this time around. "What's Eliza Dushku like?" I ask as one comes to mind.

"Eliza Dushku," Tiffany repeats like she's thinking the name aloud. "She's the young one, isn't she? A little pretty?"

"*Very*," I chuckle.

"Yes," Tiffany says, smiling and nodding, "I know exactly who you mean. I'd say Miss Dushku is *demanding*. Too many people are fussing over her and she has too many people telling her exactly what she would like to hear. The poor lamb will only ostracize herself if she isn't too careful, or lose all of her talent and simply rely on her appearance alone. No," Tiffany says as if it pains her, "Miss Dushku is certainly somebody you would have to be wary of. But anyway," she smiles, "name another. Name *anybody* you can think of!"

"Miss Lily," Samantha says, tapping her knuckles against the door as she steps into the room carrying the sandwich I didn't even ask for on a plate. "I have Lee's sandwich."

"Thank you," I say exactly as Tiffany snaps, "Well give it to the man!"

I smile, taking the sandwich and turn hungry just looking at it. Samantha asks, "Is there anything else I should do?"

"Yes," Tiffany says in a voice that makes it clear to see she's trying to hide a little anger, "get back to work and close the door behind you."

Samantha rushes out of the room and closes the door behind her. I look to my sandwich, lightly grilled vegetables and expensive spiced meat on wholemeal bread and realise I'm going to be real thirsty before I've finished this but I don't want to mention a drink for fear of getting Samantha into a little trouble for not thinking ahead.

"Is it to your liking?" Tiffany asks before I've taken a single bite out of it.

"It looks delicious," I respond.

"Good," she says. "Would you like anything else?" she asks. "Would you like me to send somebody out for a birthday cake? There is such a wonderful bakery nearby."

"No," I tell her, "this is more than enough."

"You can never have enough," Tiffany informs me. "But how about you take a hot shower once you've finished that? I can have those clothes washed and ironed for you before you have to go."

"Are you trying to nicely tell me how I smell?" I laugh.

"Not at all," she says, "you smell exactly how a man should smell but rarely does. I just want to make you comfortable, Lee. I'd just love to see you smile."

"That's good to know," I tell her, laughing a little down to nerves.

"That's what I'm talking about!" she coos. "Now come on," she says to encourage me, "name some more names and I'll let you know what they are *really* like."

32

EXTRACTOR FANS COME to life the moment I'm done showering and all of the steam I've made begins to disappear. I push my wet hair back with both hands and stepping out of the walk-in shower I take a thick cotton towel from the rail and wrap it around my waist. Only then do I see the problem regarding my clothes.

"Fuck."

Even if Tiffany has somebody place my clothing into a tumble-dryer, it's more than likely that they're still being tossed around a washing machine. So what is it I'm going to do now?

"Fuck," I mutter again. I fuck it one last time for luck or good measure before unlocking the bathroom door and step back out onto the cool landing. "Hello?" I call.

"In here," Tiffany calls back to me from one of the nearby rooms.

"This is a little embarrassing," I chuckle, "but what are we going to do about my clothes?"

"Come here and we'll talk about it."

I look down at my feet; at the water running down my legs. "I'm dripping wet."

"I have a maid," Tiffany says like that answers everything. Deciding I shouldn't care if she doesn't care, I walk away from the bathroom and call out to her again to try and have her reveal herself to me so I don't have to look inside every room before I find her. The plan works. One of the doors a little farther down opens that little bit more and Tiffany smiles at me. "In here," she says and then she turns out of sight. I head into the room to find her sitting at a desk with Mark Chambers. There's a chair, for me, I'm assuming on the other side of the desk. The only other things I see in here include a writing desk with personal computer, a small couch and a number of polished awards resting upon shelves. Another door stands ajar on the far wall but I think nothing of it.

"Lee," Tiffany smiles lighting one of her long, slim cigarettes, "you remember Mark, don't you?"

"Of course," I say and I smile at him as if to prove a point and he raises his eyebrows before looking back at the piece of paper he has in front of him, sucking on the end of a ballpoint pen as he does so.

"Take a seat," Tiffany says on placing her pack of cigarettes and lighter down on the table. "Have a cigarette," she adds. "And don't worry at all about getting the chair wet!"

I smile, take a hold of the towel around my waist for fear of it unexpectedly dropping and make my way to the chair they have offered me. "Lee," Tiffany says on looking me right in the eye, "I'm just going to tell it like it is; I want to look out for you," she claims, "I want to take care of your interests and make your life easier. I want to use the talents God gave me," she says as if to remind me of what I said to her in the back of her limousine only yesterday, "just to try and make you happy when and where I can."

"This is a contract," Chambers says on pushing the piece of paper out in front of me. "Miss Lily has already signed it," he continues and I look down at it to see what I assume to be her signature near the bottom of the page with today's date beside it. The neatly printed paragraphs and notes mean nothing to me, so I ignore them.

"If you think that doesn't look like my signature," Tiffany says to me, "it's because that is my *real* signature. I have another for when I'm signing something for the fans," she winks.

"Once you sign it," Chambers goes on, "I'll sign it to make it official."

I clear my throat. Feeling more than a little uncomfortable here, I ask, "Make *what* official?"

"My looking after you," Tiffany says.

"What Miss Lily means," Chambers explains for his client, "is she will do her best to make you happy, despite your chosen circumstances, in exchange for a little company and support. This contract," he adds tapping the end of his ballpoint pen against the paper, "simply says you will not make details concerning your friendship public knowledge."

"I don't want the press to get the wrong idea," Tiffany says to me with a smile.

"This contract," Chambers says, "is just to prove how you two have reached an agreement, and you have no intention of using Miss Tiffany Lily in a way that could cause her or her career harm and/or distress."

I know what you're thinking. You're thinking how I'm just a seventeen year old from a small, worthless town called Sinclair where the person you eventually marry is bound to be related to you already. You're thinking about how I arrived here in Los Angeles and asked a record store owner why he doesn't stock cassette tapes. You're thinking I'm as naive as they come, but even I have an idea to what Tiffany is after here… what Chambers is hoping I'll keep quiet about. But I already knew, or expected, something like this would happen and I knew it would from the moment Tiffany pushed her card in my direction. And despite this, I try to convince myself that this isn't like that at all. So I nod my head and say, "All I have to do is sign this?"

Tiffany smiles at me from across the table, "And I'll look after you like nobody ever has done before or will after."

"Sure," I say with a nonchalant shrug, "I'll sign this."

"Wonderful," Tiffany says as Chambers hands me the pen. I'm still signing and dating the document as Tiffany gets out of her chair, pecks me on the cheek and leaves the room. I slide the contract back over to Chambers and smile as I shrug my shoulders. It's a very *Now what?* kind of expression. Very calm and cool.

"If you could just walk into the next room," Chambers says on slipping the ballpoint pen back into his breast pocket, "Dr Pink would like to have just a few more minutes of your time."

"Dr Pink?"

"Don't worry," Chambers assures me, "this won't be too long or intrusive."

33

Dr Pink has me standing before him, completely naked. Down on his hands and knees, he takes a hold of my pecker and examines it real closely before paying the same delicate attention to my balls. He asks me to turn around and bend over to touch my toes and when I do, he gently parts my ass cheeks before telling me how I can put the towel back around my waist and take a seat. I do just that. Sitting opposite me, he smiles looking from me to his questionnaire and then back at me. "Just a few questions," he says without losing the friendly smile. "Don't worry," he insists, "you can't get them wrong!"

I ask him, "You don't happen to have a cigarette, do you?"

"Yes," he nods, hand dipping into his trouser pocket. "I don't smoke myself," he says pulling out an open packet of Marlboros and a box of matches, "but a lot of people I tend to work with do. You can keep those," he says as I relieve him of the cigarettes and matches and I remember the pack Tiffany has already given me and realise this has to be my lucky day. Dr Pink waits until I'm dragging smoke inside my lungs before looking back down at his questionnaire to begin.

"Have you, or anybody you have slept with, ever injected drugs?"

"No," I tell him and he ticks a box on the paper in front of him.

"Have you ever had a sexual relationship with a man?"

"No," I reply and he ticks another box.

"Have you, or anybody you have slept with, ever had a sexual relationship with an African citizen?"

"No," I say, my answer leading him to tick yet another box from that same old column.

"Have you ever had a sexually transmitted disease or infection?"

"No."

"Lucky boy," he says ticking what I assume to be the *right* box. "Have you ever suffered from hepatitis?"

"No," I smirk.

Once the list of questions is over and done with, Pink takes a blood sample and places it securely in his briefcase. He thanks me for my time and tells me he should have the blood test results come the end of the week and then he leaves me alone in the room until Tiffany comes in to join me. "I hope that wasn't too intrusive for you," she says.

"No," I smile, "just a little different."

"Good. I hope you don't mind, it's just I need to know. I need to know because the press would have a field day if they had the chance to report a new associate of mine was suffering from some terrible illness," she says and I wonder if even a small part of her believes that or whether she's fully aware of the fact she's lying. But if she is lying, is it to me or her self and what is the purpose of it?

34

Larsen opens the door of the limousine for me and I go to climb in but pause when I see the guy from the pool sitting back there. He's wearing khaki shorts with open-toe sandals and a white shirt that is open to show his toned and hairless torso. "Oh," I say before joking, "don't worry, I'll get the next one."

"Come on in," he says to me, his slender fingers easing an expensive pair of sunglasses from his pocket. "We'll drop you off wherever you want and I'll carry on. Got something to take care of," he adds as I reluctantly climb onto the nearest seat. Larsen closes the door and the guy continues, "It's all shit, you know... All of it."

I ask, "What is?"

"*This*," he says. "Tiffany doesn't have a chauffeur-driven limo twenty-four-seven. Man is hired for special events or when she wants to be seen or impress. Tiffany," he claims, "probably can't afford to have a chauffeur-driven limo sitting out front."

I remember Larsen, noticing how the vehicle is moving but manage to relax because Tiffany said drivers can't hear a thing unless you want them to. "She seems to be doing okay," I say.

"Right," he smirks. "It's all fake," he says, "it's all for show, just like she is."

"And how do you know all of this?" I ask.

"Name's Cole," he says to me with a grin, leaning over to offer me his hand. I accept it and as we shake hands he smiles real wide before continuing, "I live here. I know all the secrets," he claims, "apart from where the money is coming from. It's not like Tiffany is working regularly and for big cash."

"You live with her?"

"Sure," he says and then he swallows loudly. "It's like a prison," he tells me, "a fucking prison. Whole neighbourhood is one of those gated communities with guards. You can't leave unless you've got a card on you like the driver currently has up front.

Guards won't open the gates for you without it and if you get stopped on either side of those gates without that card, guards will bust your ass and enjoy it. A prison," he repeats, "a fucking prison."

"Where are you headed right now?"

"Me? I'm off to visit my drug dealer," he says. "What's so funny?" he asks once I start laughing.

"This doesn't sound so much like a prison," I answer.

"Don't you see?" Cole grins at me, all-knowing like. "It's the worst kind of prison that there is. You can leave whenever you want, but you know you'll always have to come back. And by the way," he says, turning to glance out of the nearest window, "I told you my name, it's only right you tell me yours. I could ask Tiffany or Chambers or even Samantha, but I don't want them to think I give a fuck."

I tell him, "My name's Lee."

"Lee," Cole snickers. "Lee is a girl's name. Somebody else back at the house must have thought the same," he says, "because they've used the fruitiest fabric softener they could find on your clothes. Where are you getting out, anyway?" he asks before I have the chance to respond to his smart-ass comment.

"Just a bus station I know."

"Is it far from here?"

"I don't know," I shrug, "maybe." I take the pack of cigarettes and the lighter from my left pocket. Cole looks at them for a second but doesn't ask for one and I refuse to offer him one seeing as he's being such a jerk. He stretches as I'm lighting up but doesn't say a thing so I do instead. "What are you getting from your dealer?" I ask.

"A little granulated happiness," Cole says. "Tiffany is trying to keep away from coke because she used to have a real bad problem with it so I take it just so she'll leave me alone. I'm guessing that's why she's so interested in you."

"What's that supposed to mean?"

"You know what it means," he laughs. "The blood test, the questions, the contract… I had all that a long time ago. But I was smarter than she thought," he says. "I got her to care for me and now I hardly ever screw her but she won't turf me out onto the streets. I've tried hitting on that Samantha a couple of times but she's making out like she isn't interested but I know she is really. Poor girl just doesn't want to lose her job. Samantha believes all the shit they feed her," he says with a yawn, "and she thinks she'll never work in showbiz again if she lets me screw her. That's all Hollywood is at all levels," he sighs. "People feeding people bullshit."

I want to say something but the only thing I can think of is what Doyle said, about Tiffany collecting *people like me*, and Cole's claim that he went through the same audition I just have some time ago. "If that's true," I finally ask him, "how can I know you're not talking shit to me right now?"

"I guess you don't," he shrugs. "But Tiffany wants you to call at the end of the week, am I right? Wants you to call about the blood test results?"

"Sure," I nod.

"Then you'll be seeing me again if you're as clean as you want them to believe. You'll see me and you'll see how I've been telling you the truth all along."

Neither one of us says a thing after that. I have the impression that Cole is leaving me to think over everything he has told me but I'm not, I'm wondering if Doyle will be back at Saint Claire's, whether he'll have brought Owen with him or if he's going to say something about how I left this morning without saying a thing and disappeared for the day. Larsen brings the limousine to a stop right by the bus station I first arrived in LA at, and not before time. I turn to Cole and say, "Well, I guess I'll see you real soon."

"Wait," he says, "one last thing, before Larsen lets you out."

"What is it?" I ask.

"I know it probably sounds like I'm just trying to spoil what looks like a good thing," he says real fast, "that I'm just trying to keep Tiffany all to myself, but that's not what I'm doing and I can prove it. Next time she's talking stars with you, make up a name," he smirks. "That's all I ask, make up a name. I used to do it *all* the time, and you know something? She had an opinion on *every* one of them!”

35

THE SUN IS as good as gone but the air is still too hot. Making my way back to Saint Claire's, I take one of the two packs of cigarettes from my pocket and return it to take out the other because I want to smoke one brand first before moving on to the next. Lighting up, I delve a hand into my back pocket to check that the card Tiffany gave me is there and it is. Whoever washed and ironed my clothes was kind enough to remove the card before washing my things and then slipped it back where they had found it. I laugh to myself on how the day has turned out and sniff at the sleeve of my shirt. It smells better than anything I have ever worn before has ever smelled. I laugh again but stop on thinking about Doyle, and how he'll react if he happens to notice just how clean and fresh I am.

"Fuck him," I mutter before pulling a little smoke into my lungs. "Fuck him," I say just to convince myself I mean it. Because if he's allowed his friends, if he's fucking allowed Owen, surely I'm allowed my own? So what if he has a problem with Tiffany Lily? It's not like he'll have to come with me when I go and see her.

Cole comes back to mind and I try to figure him out but I just can't. I wonder just how much of what he told me, if any of it, is true or whether he was just saying what somebody had told him to say. But why would he be told to say that? To see if I would still call Tiffany's number at the end of the week? Of course I'd call, I'm living on the fucking streets!

But had Cole lived on the streets? Maybe he was a struggling actor Tiffany had been introduced to. I could imagine him, being new to LA and all, and he gets introduced to Tiffany and she promises to look after him; to introduce him to the 'right' people but it's all lies. And the more I think about it, the more I think that's got to be the case… that she's 'looking after' him. I mean, he was relaxing at the side of the pool when I first set eyes on him. All his talk about it being like a prison and he can't stand the woman responsible, it was probably nothing more than him trying to exercise the old acting muscles he's allowed to go to waste and like a fool, I'd been willing to believe him.

"But not again," I sigh, tossing the end of my cigarette into the gutter.

Saint Claire's looks empty. It looks duller and somehow older but I can't explain how or why. Even before I've taken a look around the place, I can be positive Doyle isn't home yet. Or maybe he is, it's just that *home* isn't here no more. Pushing the door open wide enough for me to enter, I walk along the corridor and look for a sign that he's here but can't find one. I stop by his room and surprise, surprise he isn't to be found. The all too familiar feeling of abandonment claims me as its own.

Lighting a cigarette, I kneel down beside the gym mat he uses as a mattress and poke around his sleeping bag to see if he has anything hidden inside or around it but find nothing. *What would you prefer*, I think to myself, *Doyle staying with Owen or Owen coming to live here, with us?*

"I'm not going to dignify that with a response," I mutter to myself, turning to head to my own room before I have to stub out the cigarette I'm smoking.

36

There's a blind moment of sheer panic because I wake so suddenly and with no idea why. After a second, I realise it's the water that has woken me and I'm in the changing room of Saint Claire's. Well, the adjoining shower area to be precise. Still glued to the spot, it takes me another moment to make sense of why I'm here. It's because of a dream, I finally remember. I'd dreamt of moving back to Sinclair - moving back to the family home. It was only supposed to be for a while, only supposed to be until the apartment where I'd been staying had undergone some repairs but Uncle Nick was already pissed at having me back home. A heated argument led to him charging at me, pinning me down against the kitchen table with his fingers tightly knotted around my throat.

And I'd woken in fright soon after and stumbled into Doyle's room while lighting a cigarette, but his room was empty. Feeling so tired had only acted to increase my fears, my feeling of panic, and I had made my way down into the basement as if to hide from it all. Had I been certain Uncle Nick was in Saint Claire's as I staggered down here? I'm pretty sure I had. And I had been just as sure he would never find me down here, so I had curled up in the shower area and now, falling water has awoken me.

"Fuck," I mutter, pushing my hair out of my eyes. I wonder if the showers have gone and broken… if they're getting to release powerful blasts of water from the showerheads whenever they decide but then I hear Doyle laughing and I see him standing just a couple of feet to my left. He's completely naked, grinning down at me as he rubs a bar of soap over his body to get himself clean.

"Fuck," I say a little louder, struggling to get to my feet because everything I try and lean on for support is that slippery.

"What're you doing down here?" Doyle laughs as I stagger beyond the showerheads. He seems to be in good spirits but

I'm wondering if it could all be an act. He could have woken me before turning the water on, but he chose not to. He *chose* to entertain himself at my expense.

"I'm," I say from the changing room, dropping my eyes down to see the puddle of water I'm already standing in because I'm that wet, "fuck," I mutter. "I don't know," I call out to him. "I must have been sleepwalking or something."

"You're lucky you only came down here," Doyle says, "you could have walked out onto the street and stepped in front of a car. No driver would have stopped for you around here," he says, "they would have just carried on driving without even looking back."

"Yeah," I say before asking, "what time did you get back?"

"Just an hour ago or something," he replies. "I'm getting old," he says, "it's taking me longer to recover from drinking and I didn't even have it in me to try walking back here under yesterday's sun."

"Yeah," I agree, trying to squeeze the water from my shirt. I know I'll have to dry off and change my clothes, it's just that I'm trying to figure out the best way to tell him what I got up to during his absence. "Where's your friend?"

"Owen?" Doyle calls out as if he wants to be sure we're discussing the same person. "He's at his place."

"Thank fuck for that," I mutter to myself before loudly saying, "he didn't come back here with you?"

"No," Doyle laughs. "Owen figures he has it made just fine where he is right now."

"Oh. Anyway," I tell him, "I'm going upstairs to dry off and change my clothes."

Doyle asks me, "Before you go, do you want to know what the good news is?"

"Sure," I say, "what's the good news?"

"You won't have to worry about washing those clothes you're wearing!"

I still can't decide whether he's poking fun because he's pissed at me, still can't decide how best to tell him about my seeing Tiffany Lily again, so I leave the basement without saying another word. I take squelching footsteps that force water out of my shoes and leave soaking footprints all the way back upstairs. I consider testing just how good a mood Doyle is in by tossing my wet clothing onto his sleeping bag and gym mat he sleeps on but decide against it. Instead I walk into my room and close the door behind me. The air's refreshingly cool because of my soaked clothing but I take to undressing before they start to smell.

As carefully as I can manage, I take the card Tiffany had given me from my back pocket. It's soaked right through but the number hasn't smudged in the slightest. For a second, not a single thought crosses my mind as I stare at the card. I'm hoping I'll experience an epiphany of some kind, one that lets me know whether I should destroy the card and forget all about her or keep hold of it to see what I can get out of it, but nothing comes to mind. Nothing comes to mind at all.

I place the card atop the radiator even though it never gets warm and I start to undress.

37

THE TWO OF us are walking through one of the neighbourhoods where a few people that have a lot of time for Doyle live. It's the third, maybe fourth time we've walked around the block because we're yet to see any of them and we're hoping to catch them as they come walking out of their home. Let it look like we've all just happened to have bumped into each other, talk a while, make a few jokes, accept whatever bag of groceries they go in to get for us. I'm still undecided if Doyle has a problem with me or not, but keeping my distance from him could only make it worse so I accompany him around the streets of LA as usual. "Come on," Doyle says under his breath, rolling a coin from one finger to the next, "come on, come on, come on, where are you good people?"

I take a pack of cigarettes from my pocket and place one between my lips before holding the pack in front of Doyle. He accepts a cigarette with a nod of the head; slips the cigarette between his lips but then pulls it out to take a better look at it. "This isn't your usual brand," he says.

"Who says I have to stick to a usual brand?" I ask lighting my cigarette. I'm glad Doyle is already taking his lighter from his pocket because I keep misplacing my Zippo so I'd rather not have it out of my possession if even for a moment. Truth to be told, I have no idea why I'm so desperate to keep it with me. It's not like I associate any fond memories with it; Dad died before I had the chance to form any happy memories. Maybe I just want it as a reminder of how I finally got one over Uncle Nick when it really mattered?

"I knew somebody once," Doyle says lighting his cigarette, "who told me smoking is the longest suicide attempt you can ever try."

"Maybe," I shrug. "Do you agree with that?"

"Maybe," he shrugs.

We go on walking in silence for a while. "You know who I saw the day before yesterday?" I eventually ask.

"No," Doyle says. "Who did you see the day before yesterday?"

"Tiffany Lily," I tell him.

"Christ," he sighs, "twice in one week. Did she see you?"

"Yeah," I say. "Actually, she picked me up."

Doyle smirks. "She picked you up? What's that mean?"

"It means she picked me up," I tell him. "It was after I left you sleeping off a hangover at Owen's place. It was hot and I was tired and thirsty, and I remembered how she'd given me a card with her number on it the day before. So I called her," I explain, "and she came by to pick me up in her limo. Bought me a bottle of Dr Pepper."

"The woman is a saint," he says sarcastically.

"We went back to her place," I say, "and she let me take a shower while she had my things washed. She even had somebody make me a sandwich."

"What was on it?"

"What?" I ask in surprise.

"The sandwich." Doyle asks, "What was on the sandwich?"

"Oh," I tell him. "Spicy meat and vegetables."

"She offer you any food to bring back with you? Slip you any money?"

"No."

"Nothing at all?"

"Nothing," I tell him.

"Then she's still a cunt."

"About that," I say, "what's the deal between you two?"

"Deal?" Doyle says, "There's no *deal* between me and Tiffany Lily."

"It seems like you don't think much of her," I say as we turn the corner, preparing to walk the full length of the block once more.

"This is LA," Doyle smirks. "I don't think much of most people here."

"I guess," I say and I act like I'm going to let it drop but in the end I ask, "have you ever slept with her? With Tiffany, I mean."

"No," he answers me with a laugh. "I've seen a couple of pictures of her," he says, "back when she first started acting, when she was around sixteen, seventeen. She looked great back then, she really did. But she went and lost it all," he says, "like she was the ugly duckling in reverse."

"Well," I say like it's nothing important, "I think she wants to sleep with me."

"She probably does."

"No," I tell him, "I'm not just saying that, I really mean it."

"And I believe you."

"But you don't understand! She had a doctor examine me and take a blood sample. My results will be in by the end of the week."

"And she wants you to call her around then?"

"Yes," I say, "at least, that's what she said I should do."

Doyle nods, takes one final pull on his cigarette and flicks the end at the gutter but misses. "It sounds to me like she wants to fuck you," is all he can say to that.

"Do you think I should?"

"What're you asking me for?" Doyle laughs. "Are you hoping I'll tell you how you won't go to Hell if you fuck her before marriage or something? You know," he says, "I never could understand why God would care about something like that."

"It's not that," I say. "It's just… It's just she was saying how she'd like to look after me. I think she was offering, you know, a little money or something in exchange for sex."

Doyle shrugs his shoulders. "Prostitution is the oldest business the world has in it."

"But do you *think* I should go through with it?"

Doyle sighs. "I don't know why you're asking me," he says, "or what it is exactly you want to hear. Only you can answer this one. It's all about self-worth, I guess. I'm not saying you should look down on yourself if you go through with it, because it could make your life a lot easier if she's willing to throw money in your direction. The real issue is whether you can stomach being around her for so long."

"I don't think she's so bad," I tell him.

"Well," Doyle says to me, "I guess that's more than half the battle already won."

38

TIFFANY'S RACK LOOKS great up until she gets on her back. Soon as that happens, the old girls appear to stand too far apart, like you could place a truck tyre between them. Despite the work she's had done on her face to try and stand firm against signs of ageing, and up close, you can see faint, almost invisible marks where a surgeon's knife may have made a small cut, you can see faint wrinkles upon her skin when you're close enough to kiss her. But her stomach is the strangest to me and again, I'm guessing it's all down to surgery. The skin looks as if it has been pulled tight; so tight in fact that the abdominal muscles underneath look dangerously close to tearing clean through it.

But we continue to kiss anyway and I try to convince myself that it's all worth while, if not for the money I could get but for the fact that I'm about to pork a star. Just a few hours earlier, I found out my HIV/AIDS test came back negative. It came back negative and I should have *known* that it would seeing how I've only ever slept with one person, the wonderful Eleanor Gayle, and we always used protection. But when I called Tiffany earlier today and she sent Larsen to pick me up from the bus station, I was a little scared. I was scared the blood test would come back as positive and I would be handed a death sentence. Instead, I feel like I've been given a second chance. And now I'm celebrating the potential seventy or so years left ahead of me by jumping into bed with a star. For money.

Tiffany Lily has satin sheets and the pillows are thick with duck feathers. Her bed is huge, one of those with four tall posts of the finest wood and silk curtains hanging down to make it look like it should be in some rich oil sheik's pleasure room. The venetian blinds are drawn but enough natural light remains for me to see the room in detail, as well as Tiffany's many, many flaws. I even see the framed *Son of Kong* movie poster on the wall and admit to myself I'll never be able to watch that movie in the same way as long as I live. Even if I have eighty or so years left ahead of me…

"Oh baby," Tiffany says again. She seems to say that every time I do something new and it's a little off-putting. "Oh baby," she says again, and then she asks me to venture down south for her but I make out like I didn't hear her. She takes my face in her hands and kisses me, looks me square in the eyes and says, "Won't you?"

"Won't I *what*?" I ask like I don't know what it is she's after.

"Cunnilingus," she smiles. "You do know what that is, don't you?"

"Sure," I smile back at her. I used to eat Eleanor's pussy quite a lot. I really liked it to begin with but then I got onto the fact she wasn't going to return the favour, but I carried on doing it anyway, hoping she would feel guilty and give me head one day, but it never happened. But like an idiot, I continued to please Eleanor with my tongue and maybe it was the feeling I was getting the short straw, maybe I just took a real disliking to doing it, but I would have to discreetly pull and stroke at my boner or risk losing it. I'm serious. Old boy must have been holding some kind of protest!

But anyway, I reluctantly take to kissing Tiffany's neck ("Oh baby") and work my way down, real slow, kissing her chest and then her stomach, flickering my tongue here and there with hopes she'll really like it and then I'll be able to delay the inevitable for a little while longer. Unfortunately, it doesn't appear to be working and I reach her naval. Tiffany moans with pleasure, presses her head down into those luxury pillows of hers and takes a tight hold of the bedspread. Admitting defeat, I slope down to where she has wanted me to be all along and she spreads her legs as wide as they'll go. I take one last look at her and then get to work. She's moaning right away whereas I'm trying to figure out what her taste reminds me of. The best I can think of is gammon but that doesn't sit right for some reason. She clearly tastes of gammon, I *know* she tastes of gammon, but I can't accept it.

She moans louder. In the back of my mind, I thank those

old sex movies of Uncle Nick's for showing me how to do this to a woman. I mean, women have it so much easier on their end. They want to give head, they give head. It's all there for them to see, clear as crystal. But a woman's parts are all hidden away, like it's some mystery we men have to work out if we want an easy life. Tiffany's even looks pretty different to the way Eleanor's looks, so I can't help but wonder if maybe she had a little surgery down here, too.

Tiffany moans *real* loud and I can't help but remember what Cole told me, about how he's been holding out on her when it comes down to making the beast with two backs. I can't help but hope, no, I pray, this lack of excitement for her will have her reaching an orgasm within a matter of moments and I'll be free to resurface because of it. She moans all the more, gives an involuntary leg spasm and I'm convinced everything is going to work out for me yet.

"Don't mind me," Cole says on walking straight into the room, "I just want to grab a shirt."

"Fuck!" Tiffany yelps in surprise, kicking me square in the face. I tumble from the bed and stay where I land in a desperate attempt to hold on to at least some dignity. I watch as Cole, wearing tight blue shorts and a necklace and sunglasses but nothing else, opens the door of the walk-in-wardrobe and disappears from view. I hear wire hangers being moved along a rail from in there. "Tiffany," he calls, "have you seen my blue shirt?"

"Damn you, Cole!" Tiffany screams, "Damn you!"

"What?" He calls back, "I'm off to see a friend! I thought you'd appreciate me getting out of your hair like this!"

39

We're standing in the tall grass behind Saint Claire's because it's yet another hot night and we're desperate to cool down. I'm looking at how the grass is barely moving because the breeze is that weak, and I'm wondering how many rats are scurrying around us and how close they're coming. There's an old refrigerator somebody dumped here just a dozen or so feet away and I wonder if that's where the rats sleep or whether they go underground. Doyle takes a long drag on the joint he's holding. Some bum turned up at Saint Claire's the night before last and found us in the kitchen area. Once he realised we weren't hired security (which was almost immediately) he asked if there was room for him to stay a while and when Doyle said it all depended on what he was willing to contribute, he handed over a bag of green. At first I thought it was a sign of how desperate he was, but the green is pretty shit. It's clearly been mixed with a lot of garbage so it looks like there's more than there really is and the guy that handed it over, Kyle or something his name is, is probably glad to be shot of it. Of course, neither one of us have told Kyle about the hot water or the showers down in the basement.

"So," Doyle says on holding the smoke in his lungs for a little longer, "have you screwed her yet?"

"Why do you want to know?" I ask.

"Curious," he says, releasing smoke from his lungs. "Have you?"

"Yes," I tell him. What I don't tell him is how I practically ejaculated the moment I was inside of her. That was embarrassing enough, trying to explain to Tiffany how it was probably down to my being *out of practice* without Doyle knowing all about it. Without Doyle knowing how Tiffany had taken it as a compliment before handing me a bottle of Viagra from a bedside drawer to help me make amends. And I don't get Viagra, I really don't. You shoot your load but the boner remains. You can shoot your load a number of times, an amount of liquid that gets sparser and sparser, but you remain hard as nails. Your stomach muscles are cramping over, you're so worn out you can hardly breathe.

Understandably, the woman is having the time of her life, but for the man? No… I just don't get Viagra.

Doyle laughs a little. "Young man," he says like it's real funny, "I hope you remembered to use a condom."

Of course we did. Tiffany has a lot of them in an old shoebox underneath her bed and I mean *a lot*. A whole variety of them including ribbed, dotted, ribbed and dotted, ultra thin, extra lubricated, extra thick. I consider making a joke to Doyle, a joke about wearing a ribbed condom inside-out for my own pleasure, but decide against it. Instead I just try and remember which one of them I wore that first time. It was probably *ribbed* in a desperate attempt to impress even though I don't really believe that ribbed condoms make a real difference for a woman. I think that it's nothing more than a marketing trick, have the man gain a little extra confidence or earn brownie points by making it look like he cares about the woman's needs.

"Here you go," he says handing me the joint I'm only all too happy to accept despite how it tastes like shit. With a little luck, it'll help me sleep through another unbearably hot night. "So when're you seeing her again?"

"I don't know," I shrug. "When I next call her."

"Bet you're real glad we don't have a telephone," Doyle smirks. "Keeps you in charge, right?" He asks me, "Has she offered to buy you a cellphone?"

"Yeah," I say pulling back on the joint. The end lights up, ash moves along as paper makes delicate crackling noises and a vile and heavy taste floods my mouth. "I said it would be a waste of money," I add, just to let some of the bad taste jump out of my mouth.

Doyle grins and lightly kicks at something in front of him that I can't make out because of the thick grass. "You Sinclair boys," he says, "are nothing but heartbreakers. Wanting to buy you a cellphone already," he chuckles. "She given you anything else yet?"

"No," I say on shaking my head. "She has somebody make me a bite to eat when I'm there. Lets me have a hot shower before and after, but that's pretty much all so far."

"At least you're getting your nuts. If you're not planning on seeing her tomorrow," he says, "do you want to get some supplies in? We're almost completely out of Valium," he explains, "and there's next to no beer left." He spits before adding, "I think our uninvited guest may have taken some but I'm not too sure about it."

"Sure," I nod, "it sounds like a plan."

"Good," Doyle says looking off to the horizon, "we'll try and get a little food, too."

I nod, take one last drag on the joint before passing it back and ask, 'How long is he going to be staying with us, anyway?"

"I don't know," Doyle shrugs, "until the grass he handed over as payment runs out."

"It's shitty grass," I say, "it'll probably last quite a while."

"You're probably right," Doyle says, looking down at the joint between his fingers. "I'll see what I can do about moving him along," he sighs.

<h1 style="text-align:center">40</h1>

Cole sees me standing at the bus station and honks the horn of the brand new BMW he's driving and pulls it to a stop nearby. I look to the road for a moment, just to be sure no black limousine is following behind, and then make my way to the waiting BMW. I climb into the passenger seat and slam the door shut behind me. I'm still fastening my seatbelt as Cole pulls back onto the road and takes to racing along, overtaking the nearest car ahead. "This car," he says, "has some serious thunder."

"This yours?" I ask him.

"Tiffany's," he says, "but I think she's only renting it for a while."

"Oh," I say. "Where's Larsen? I thought he'd be picking me up."

Cole shakes his head. "Tiffany has an audition today, doctor's wife on a daytime drama, so Larsen's taking her there. What can I say?" Cole smirks, "You must have been accepted if she's no longer sending a limo out for you all the time… It's like you're about to see how they're really only for special occasions, like I told you a while back?"

I nod my head and light a cigarette. I offer Cole a smoke and he accepts. "You know how long Tiffany will be gone?"

"Couple of hours yet," Cole replies, "but don't you worry about getting bored. I'm just on my way to pick up a little coke," he says, "and then we'll drive back to Tiffany's place and sit around the pool drinking cocktails."

"Sounds like a plan," I tell him. "Are you still doing coke so Tiffany won't try getting too close?"

"Are you kidding? Thanks to you, she hasn't tried anything with me for a while. Doesn't even ask me to spoon her, but I do wish she'd at least have the sheets changed after the two of you have been fucking," he says. "You have her making them wetter than a waterbed with a puncture."

I laugh. "What can I say?" I tell him, "I do my best."

"Yeah," Cole sighs, "but I've a feeling I'm going to have to start being sweet with her again. It's the reason for the coke," he claims, "make it seem like a good idea to get frisky with her. No offence."

"Don't worry about it," I smirk. "But what has you thinking that again?"

"Thinking *what* again?"

"That you'll have to go back to screwing her."

"Oh," Cole nods, "yeah, I get you. Well," he begins, "don't get me wrong. I've been happy that she's been well and truly distracted so she leaves me be. I don't know if you've noticed, but me and Samantha have been growing real close, too…"

I can't say I've noticed.

"But something happened just the other day," he goes on, "and it's got me worried. I'd taken a dip in the pool, showered off, and I went into the bedroom and put on a nice shirt. But Tiffany," he says, "Tiffany saw me wearing it and went crazy. I'd no idea what was up with her, whether she was back on the drink or if she'd just been told she hadn't got a part or something, but then she told me the shirt I had put on was *your* shirt. Your shirt," he grins, dragging smoke deep inside of his lungs. "Did you know she's buying you clothes?"

"Yeah," I say with a nod, "but she keeps them in the wardrobe for me to wear at the house or when I'm out with her. That way," I explain, "I won't make a mess of them out on the streets."

"I'm telling you," Cole says, "as soon as I saw how angry she got at me for wearing something of yours, I got a little scared. I mean," he says, "she realises she doesn't need me around any more, she could toss me out of the house and there's no way I'm going back home. So I'm going to sweet-talk her and more again. You don't mind," he asks, "do you? I'm not setting out to make her lose interest in you, nothing like that at all. Trust me, Tiffany will be more than happy to have me on some days and you on the others. She thinks she's a big enough star to have two or more men on the go."

"As long as we both remain on the easy road," I tell him, "I haven't got any problem at all with what you have to do."

We stop at Cole's dealer's place and Cole hands two fifties and a twenty over for a bag of white powder that looks unbelievably small to me and then we drive back to Tiffany's place, the guards manning the barriers nearby letting us pass the minute Cole shows them a card he takes from the dashboard. "Assholes," he says once we're driving away from them. Back at the empty house, we change into our swimming trunks and sit beside the pool with a bottle of beer each. Cole goes inside, brings out a portable stereo and turns a record on really loud. "You ever heard this?" he asks.

"I don't think so," I tell him. "Who is it?"

"The Brian Jonestown Massacre," Cole replies, clicking his fingers as he sways his hips to the music. "They're fucking mind-blowing, aren't they?"

"They sound pretty good," I agree.

"Frontman is a genius," Cole says on sitting back down beside me. He takes a silver vial from his pocket and unscrews the top, which doubles as a spoon and dips it inside to load the spoon with a little coke. He takes it to his nose and inhales, loads the spoon a second time and inhales again. He asks me, "You want some blow? This is good stuff… Real rocket fuel."

"Sure," I say with a smile, accepting the vial from him. "Thanks."

"No problem," Cole says.

"It sure is quiet here," I say. "Where is everybody?"

"Maids don't work today. Chambers and my Samantha have headed to Hollywood with Tiffany."

I snort a spoonful of white powder and offer the vial back but Cole tells me to take a little more so I do. "Do you think she'll get the part?"

"Let's hope so," Cole says. "I've already told you all of this? I don't know how she's kept hold of it for this long."

41

WE'RE SURE THE house is empty because we've been watching it pretty close the last few days, learning the homeowner's routine and whatnot. I sneak around the back and Doyle knocks at the front door. With him waiting out front, I force a window and climb inside. He stands out front just in case I have to smash glass or force a door. I mean, if you hear the sound of a breaking window or what could just be the door being forced off its hinges over at your neighbour's place but you look out and see a church Father there, you're not going to investigate, especially if you see the Father smiling a moment later and stepping on into the home. You just assume the noise was coming from elsewhere and forget all about it. You forget all about it until your neighbour calls by a few hours later to ask if you've seen or heard anything because they've been robbed.

Standing near the window I've just climbed into, I stand perfectly still for a moment and concentrate on the sound of my breathing. I *know* the house is empty but I still listen out for sounds made by another soul. I notice how my hand is pressed against the window sill and quickly move it away. I keep meaning to pick up a pair of gloves like Doyle has but keep forgetting. My fingerprints find the door handle as I leave the room, quickly making my way to the front. There's a large panel of glass in the heart of the front door. Frosted glass. I can see Doyle waiting for me to let him in, all wavy and distorted.

I let him in and he quickly closes the door behind him. "You want the top or the bottom?" he asks.

"Whatever's easiest," I say and he heads straight up the stairs. "Guess I'm bottom," I say turning back to investigate the room I'd already left behind. The first time we robbed like this, I barfed real bad in the homeowner's bathroom and not all of it made it into the toilet. I felt so guilty I wanted to leave a note as way of apology but Doyle just laughed and told me not to be so stupid.

We do this because we have to. The people that used to be only too happy to give us something to eat and expected nothing in return no longer do that. They try to avoid us, seem a little ashamed when we corner them and get to talking and they know they can't hand anything over to us. Doyle blames the economy. Doyle says the real criminals aren't breaking into houses like we are, he says they're in Washington and their homes have all kinds of advanced security systems to keep people out. "Proof Capitalism could never work," he'll say. "We should have followed the teachings of Jesus a little closer."

Rooting through the drawers of somebody's front room with my heart pounding fast, I can't help but think of my other life… The times I'm with Tiffany and I'm wearing stupidly expensive clothes. I'm glad Doyle has never seen me wearing those clothes; glad Tiffany says I can't wear them when I'm not with her because I'll only ruin them or have some punk try and lift them from me. And ever since she's been back on TV, she's been all too happy to throw money at me. Well, at *us* seeing as Cole is trying his best with her again. I was a little worried at first; worried that she'd have no use for me once he started playing with her again, but it hasn't turned out like that. Tiffany told me, in confidence of course, how Cole refuses to perform oral sex on her. Knowing that's what I have over him, I now do it for her all of the time. I've even done it during her *magic days* a couple of times. And the head she gives is phenomenal, it really is. She does this thing, where she scrapes her bottom teeth down the shaft and every single time she does it I-

"Two minutes left," Doyle calls from upstairs. "This is your first warning!"

I snap myself out of it and get back to focusing on the job at hand. Seeing a smiling lady looking down at me with her child from a framed photograph, I swallow and turn the frame so it's facing the other way so I won't have to look at them. "Fuck," I mutter, racing out to the kitchen because there's nothing for me to take here. TVs and DVD players draw too much attention if you're carrying them around without their original packaging. Bankcards still excite me whenever I see them, even though I know we can't use them. But the kitchen can be a real goldmine. We took a food processor one time; hadn't even left the neighbourhood and we'd sold it for $20 to some kid sitting on the stoop outside his place. He said his mom would love it.

"One minute," Doyle calls from upstairs. "This is your second warning so quit your grinnin' and drop your linen!"

"Fuck," I mutter rummaging around through a complete stranger's drawers. There's no food processor, no nice-looking coffee pot. Just a bulky microwave that looks like it was old in the 1980s and a dishwasher that may be a real treasure chest but I'm stuck here without the key.

"Thirty seconds," Doyle calls as he comes running down the stairs. "Last warning, here I come!"

"Fuck," I say, pocketing an open carton of cigarettes and taking an electric carver from the cutlery drawer. Doyle races into the kitchen carrying a suitcase he must have found under a bed upstairs. "You get anything?" he asks.

"Not a lot," I say. "You?"

"Couple of CDs," he says on holding the suitcase up for me to see in case I somehow missed it, "DVD player from one of the bedrooms, electric toothbrush, couple of razors and everything they had in the medicine cabinet."

Believe me, people are always willing to buy shit like razors for next to nothing. You steal them enough and it all adds up.

I ask him, "You think you could fit another DVD player in there? There's one in the next room."

"Nah," he says fishing his cigarettes and lighter from his pocket, "you have to leave them with something."

I nod my head, light a cigarette of my own to steady my nerves. "We leaving through the front or out the back?"

"Let's head out the back for a change," he says with a smile. "Enjoy the scenic route."

42

TIFFANY TAKES US (me, her, Cole, Samantha and Chambers) to a very fancy restaurant to celebrate my twenty-third birthday - which is in fact my eighteenth. It's unbelievable to be sitting at a table in such a place when, hours earlier, I had been feigning an epileptic fit on the floor of a drugstore so Doyle could grab some prescription pills and the money from the cash register while I kept everybody there distracted. I'm wearing nothing but black, a colour I've claimed as my own when I'm not around Doyle. My shirt cost over one hundred dollars. You don't want to know how much money the jeans, shoes, or cologne cost. Even the socks and underwear I've got on cost more than a reasonable pair of sneakers. What's real funny to me is how Cole has taken to dressing in nothing but white if we're leaving the mansion. Around the pool or visiting his dealer, he'll wear light clothing but if we're heading out together, he insists on nothing but white. It must look like I'm trying to be his evil clone or something.

"Well," Tiffany says with a warm smile as she raises her glass of champagne once the latest autograph-hunter leaves us all to our celebration, "we're not just here to celebrate Lee's birthday, oh no. We're also here to celebrate the fact he's been in our exclusive circle for a year now. And what a year," she boasts. "I've been nominated for six television awards and won more than half. The show is continuing to attract huge viewing figures and has been sold to almost every country around the world."

"Chambers," Cole smirks raising his own glass, "continues to annoy each and every one of us in equal measure." We all chuckle at that. Chambers laughs and flicks Cole the bird. Cole, who is sure to fuck Tiffany whenever she wants to be fucked, which is often, and just as sure to only take cocaine when she isn't able to see him do so.

"And Samantha," I say, raising my own glass, "who silently

keeps all of our shit together." Samantha blushes on hearing that. Cole does that grin he has only for her; a grin that makes it painfully obvious to see how he'd love to wrap an arm around her and pull her close but he doesn't dare in case Tiffany reacts badly to it and fires Samantha as soon as she has a reason to. Any reason. Even I sometimes wonder if I've gone and fallen in love with Samantha. She's beautiful, kind, warm… everything you struggle to find out here in Los Angeles. And best of all, she'd struggle to believe it if you told her. She's one of those rare diamonds who believes she's *nothing special* when she really is.

"Can I just add," Chambers says raising his glass, "that Tiffany's more popular than ever. Her Myspace page still has way over one million friends. *Myspace*," he makes a point of adding, "which is dying a slow death but people carry on joining it just to add her. I've read a lot of the messages she receives," he grins. "A lot of people look up to her while a lot of people, well… Let's say they want to get *romantic* with her."

"How am I doing on Facebook?" Tiffany wants to know.

"You've got a lot of people following a lot of pages dedicated to you *and* the show," Chambers happily informs her. Informs *us*.

Tiffany smiles, lowering her glass as she forgets the reason why she raised it in the first place, which was to toast my special occasion. "Are publishers still chasing me for my memoirs?"

"Yes," Chambers excitedly tells her. "I think we should get to work on it in the next five to six months. Once they're done," he smiles, "we'll welcome a bidding war from all the top names."

"I won't have to write all of it, will I?"

"No," Doyle assures her, "we'll get a ghost-writer in. Once that's selling," he says, "and if the ghost-writer is easy enough to get on with, we'll start releasing works of fiction with your name running down the spine. I think we could release two books per year and have you at the top of all the bestseller lists without even breaking a sweat."

"You really think so?" Tiffany asks in amazement.

"Trust me," Chambers smiles, "you're lightning in a bottle."

"Wow," Tiffany says, "I'd sure like to have the Noble Prize

for literature in my Media Room… To us," she says raising her glass, "and to another year as wonderful - if not better - than this one."

43

I'M BACK AT the family home, living there until I get a little money together, and I'm sitting at the kitchen table with my teeth falling out. There's no blood but my teeth are falling apart and dropping from my mouth, scattering all over the table. I try nailing my teeth back together, try forcing them back into smooth gums but they just fall back out again. I try and try again to force my badly repaired teeth back into place but they refuse to stay in my mouth.

Uncle Nick comes back home from wherever he has been all day, wearing his preaching shirt, and he screams about the mess I'm making of his kitchen and attacks me. He has me out of the chair and on the floor within seconds, kicking me as he screams words I can't really make out.

I wake with a start. Tiffany is sound asleep next to me. Cole is sleeping soundly next to her. The digital clock says it's a little after three in the morning. The room is dark but not dark enough to stop me from making out my immediate surroundings. I sit up, swing my feet onto the bedroom floor and feel around the floor in search of my discarded underwear. Finding them, I pull them up and take the pack of cigarettes and Zippo lighter from the bedside table before leaving the room. Quiet as a mouse, I creep downstairs and pour myself a tall glass of chilled orange juice before lighting a cigarette. I drain the contents of the glass and refill it. The orange juice is pretty expensive but it's not me buying it. Looking out through the patio doors, I look up to the full moon and wonder why it appears to be further away than usual. It doesn't look particularly big for a full moon.

Clearing my throat, I enter the code that deactivates the security alarm so I can open the patio doors and step outside. The air is cool and inviting. Stopping beside the pool, I dip my toes into the water and quickly pull them back because it's so unexpectedly cold. And I think of Doyle and wonder if he knows how I can turn off the alarm system here. He's never once asked me to lift something from Tiffany's place; never once asked me to take a little money from her purse.

"What's up?" Cole asks on stepping outside to join me. He's completely naked unless you count the platinum bracelet he's wearing.

"Nothing," I say, "just a bad dream. I didn't wake you, did I?"

"I'm a light sleeper," he says. "You have a spare smoke?"

"Yeah," I say handing him the Zippo and the cigarettes. He takes a cigarette, lights up and then hands my possessions back over to me. I try sliding them into a pocket and when I can't, I look down and remember how I'm only in my underwear.

"I'm too tired," Cole says as he rubs at his eyes.

"Go back to bed." I tell him, "I'll lock up."

"I'm up now," he says, "and will stay someplace between being awake and being asleep until I get a couple of lines of coke."

I ask, "You fresh out?"

"Yeah," he says, "and I don't know why. I think Tiffany might be flushing some of my shit. Seriously," he laughs, "fucking TV star with a dislike for coke? Makes no sense, does it?"

"I guess not," I reply. "You told me a long time ago," I remind him, "she used to have a problem with it."

"So I've been told," Cole says, taking a quick drag on his cigarette. "She wasn't using when I met her. Chambers told me she had to have her nose repaired, that's how bad her problem was."

I suddenly picture the three-way we had been involved in just a few short hours ago and laugh a little. What's funny is Tiffany was on her back and I was tapping her vagina and Cole was screwing her mouth. Tiffany was moaning, her eyes closed due to the pleasure she was experiencing and Cole looked to me and started making these real funny faces. At the time, I nearly choked for holding back the urge to laugh. It got even worse once I tried pulling my own humorous faces back at Cole. You have to wonder what Tiffany would have thought if she had only opened her eyes and saw us. Cole had finished by depositing his milky payload right into Tiffany's mouth, which is how he likes to bring things to an end. It's weird because I look forward to doing just that whenever Tiffany is giving me head but as soon as I ejaculate, I'm overcome with a feeling of shame and disgust for a couple of seconds. I have to go and get her a glass of water before I can kiss her again. Oh, and I have to get her a hand-towel because Tiffany *never* swallows if she can avoid it these days. Tiffany hocks the sperm into the palm of her hand and holds it there like it's loose change until she's given a towel to wipe her hands clean on. Sperm is supposed to be mostly protein and vital nutrients but Tiffany says swallowing it can see you putting on a little unwanted weight.

Cole yawns. "Man," he says, "am I beat."

I nod. "Tiffany's filming in a couple of hours, isn't she?"

"Yeah," Cole smirks. "I don't know if she'll manage to keep her eyes open," he says, "what with the pummelling we gave her."

I laugh. Cole raises a hand for a high-five I gladly give him. "Your cigarette is burning away," he says.

"Oh," I say, looking down at it. I flick off the trail of dead ash before taking it back to my lips. "Can I ask you something?"

"Go right ahead," he says, "bro."

"What was your childhood like?" I ask.

Cole shrugs and flicks his cigarette into the pool, knowing full well the pool cleaner will be fishing it out within a matter of hours. "I guess it was pretty easy for me," he says. "We didn't have any fear of a Red Invasion, something like 9/11 could never be thought possible and the only enemy we had worth mentioning was Saddam. Saddam lived out in the fucking desert and was happy pushing his own people around. Is that what you mean?"

"Sure," I shrug. "Why not?"

44

Doyle lights a cigarette, turns and shouts out to me, "You see anything?"

"No," I call back to him. We're up on the roof of Saint Claire's because there's a bad leak whenever it rains all of a sudden. I don't know what he's planning on doing if he finds it, it isn't like he has the money or tools needed to repair it but I've followed him up onto the roof anyway and being up here on the roof, I've learned something… I'm scared of heights. Doyle's been walking all over without giving a damn whereas I'm practically frozen to the spot. I take baby-steps every couple of seconds but that's it. To Doyle, it probably looks like I'm just determined not to walk past a hidden crack or hole that lets the rain in and look an idiot because of it.

"Fuck," Doyle says. "Fuck," he says a second time.

It's only rained real heavy a couple of times but there's already a bad smell coming from upstairs because of it. Doyle's worried that the water might blow the electricity we have or lead to an electrical fire, just like he's worried we could end up with serious breathing problems if we don't manage to stay on top of the damp/mould/mildew issues. I keep telling him if mould kicks in as bad as he thinks it might, at least we'll have access to penicillin whenever we need it. We scrape a little into jam jars and we could maybe sell it. Organic produce is all the rage.

"I don't like it," Doyle says with a shake of his head, "I don't like it at all."

"Me neither," I say, only I'm talking about being up on the roof.

"Fuck," Doyle says, chuckling to himself as he looks off into the distance. "You have got to be kidding me!"

I ask, "What is it?" because I'm too scared to take enough steps over in his direction to get a good look at whatever it is he can see.

"Owen," he says. "It's fucking Owen!"

"Owen?" I ask, "The black dude with AIDS?"

"Yeah," Doyle laughs. "Owen."

"Where?"

"Heading this way!" Doyle laughs and then he cups his hands around his mouth and yells, "Owen!" before waving and laughing. He turns and asks me, "What the fuck is Owen doing out here?"

"I don't know."

"Fuck," he says, "we'd best go down and see him!"

"Yeah," I say, "we'd best," and I'm relieved at the idea of climbing back down but terrified at the same time. I don't want to lose my footing when I'm climbing back in through the window because I could break my fucking neck hitting the ground.

"Come on," Doyle laughs, flicking his cigarette away without a care in the world as he starts climbing back down like it's supposed to be this easy. I take a couple of deep breaths, dangle myself down from the ledge and stretch my legs out until one of them is on the window-ledge beneath. How Doyle is already inside, I'll never fucking know. I'm still unsure to how I managed to climb out here to begin with! But I ease myself down, keeping a tight hold of the nearest drainpipe, and soon I'm kneeling in the open window and I release the drainpipe at the exact same moment I jump forward before I have the slightest chance of falling back. I bang my knee on the classroom floor pretty badly but I still mutter a silent *thank you* to God and kiss the filthy, tiled floor. With a limp, I make my way out of the room as quickly as I can and hobble down the staircase.

Doyle's already standing at the entrance when I reach him and Owen is only a couple of feet away from the door. Owen, who now looks like a skeleton with cheap leather for skin, is all smiles despite how bad he looks. It looks like he shouldn't even be able to walk unaided, let alone carry the bags loaded with his worthless possessions.

"Well, well, well," Owen pants, "aren't you both a sight for sore eyes?"

Owen drops his bags at the door and Doyle hugs him. "Jesus," Doyle laughs, "what're you doing here?"

"I remembered the invite you gave me," Owen replies. "Thought I'd come and see if Saint Claire's is as flush as you made it out to be." He turns to me and asks, "How're you doing, Lee?"

"I'm good," I say, offering him my hand instead of a warm embrace. "How about you?"

"Up and down. Had to leave my place," he says more to Doyle than to me. "Some developer or something bought the land. They're tearing the building down to make luxury apartments with a state of the art gym in the basement."

Doyle smirks. "Who can afford that nowadays?" he asks.

"You know how it is," Owen shrugs. "There'll always be yuppies with money. But this," he says raising his eyes, "is Saint Claire's, huh? The church and residential palace of Father Doyle himself…"

"Hardly a palace," I correct him.

"Roof is leaking," Doyle says as if desperate to explain my remark. "You notice that funky smell?"

Owen shakes his head from side to side. "Can't say I do," he says.

"We can," Doyle sighs. "We've had heavy rain followed by the sun. Place is going to be full of mould if we're not careful."

Owen laughs. "Mould is nothing to be too concerned about," he says. "You saw the last place I was staying at!"

"That place didn't look too bad," Doyle lies.

"Well, it was," Owen says. "I'm sort of happy to be out of the place. I can't say I'll miss the neighbours."

"Where are you staying now?" I ask him.

"Well," Owen says, "here - if there's still room going to spare."

"For you," Doyle says, "we'd make room."

45

Cole and I are supposed to be watching Tiffany film a couple of vital scenes for the TV drama she's in but we're mostly hanging out way behind the crew, helping ourselves to the classy food that's available in the studio. The first few times I came to the studio and saw how what I had assumed to be a large room in a house up on Hollywood was nothing more than three walls and well-placed furniture, it was so surreal… Like you can't believe what you see or hear out in Los Angeles. Now I come out here and watch them move one set of scenery after another. Cole makes himself another open sandwich to go with his Diet Coke and asks me, "Have you tried the sushi?"

"No," I tell him.

"Try the sushi," Cole insists. "It's really good."

"No," I say, "I read a lot of people die of food poisoning in Japan because of sushi."

Cole laughs. "Where did you read that?" he asks.

"I can't remember. It was in a magazine some old lady had in her house, back in the town where I grew up. I flicked through it when I was taking a break from tiling her bathroom walls."

We turn back around, look beyond the cameras and the lighting and the runners and the director and everybody else. We look straight to Tiffany, filming her 'explosive' scene with Gunnar Marsden. He plays her adopted son but they're soon to become lovers in an upcoming storyline because Gunnar has a *lot* of fans, so they're giving him better storylines to try and keep him from looking for movie roles.

A lot of people are tipping Gunnar to be the next James Bond, which is pretty ironic. I say it's ironic because Gunnar is homosexual and Bond hates homosexuals. Of course, only a small number of people know that Gunnar is queer. Sometimes I wonder if the hot model he lives with knows he is or not. She sometimes turns up to watch the shooting but she's having her picture taken for Vogue or something today.

"Look at him," Cole says lighting a cigarette. "You think I'd be bedding men if I had his looks?"

"Haven't you listened to a single word Tiffany has said? Practically every actor that has made a big name for himself in television is queer."

"That's what they *want* her to think," he smirks.

"Hey," some youngster, probably on work experience or something says to Cole appearing at his side, "you can't smoke here!"

Cole says, "I can't?"

"No," the kid snaps. "Put your fucking coffin-nail out already," he says. Coffin-nail. People are so health conscious out here when it comes to smoking cigarettes but they're popping prescription pills or worse every five minutes.

Cole sighs. "I'll put it out," he says, "but that'd mean going for a walk so I could have another and I don't know if I'd bother coming back. See her?" he asks on pointing a finger in Tiffany's direction, "I'm with her, if you get what I mean? I go missing," he warns, "she'll worry and filming will have to be stopped until somebody finds me. Believe me, when I come back, I'll make no secret of the fact you chased me out of here. I might even say you offered a deal, you were only going to let me go on smoking here if I sucked your dick or something like that."

Even Tiffany is taken aback at how popular she has become since first getting the part. The producers *know* she is the biggest female star they have right now. And Tiffany knows so, of course, both Cole and I know. So Cole can issue such threats to get what he wants whenever we're out here. The kid silently thinks over the information he's just been handed, turns his lips into a thin line and turns to walk away with his fists clenched. "Yeah," Cole mutters turning back to the table of food, "get the fuck out of here."

I ask, "Are you going to tell her about him?"

"If he shoots me any funny looks before the day is out, sure. I'll even tell her how we heard him bitching about her."

"Yeah," I grin, "I heard him referring to her as 'washed-up.'"

"I heard him say a lot worse. Anyway," Cole asks, "has Tiffany told you about the upcoming vacation?"

"No," I say, "what vacation is this?"

"They're stretching this whole *forbidden love* story out to get as much press coverage as possible," Cole explains, "and that means Tiffany's character disappearing for a while to try and resist him… She runs off to a convent or something, so Tiffany's looking into holidaying in France during her absence. Maybe even Italy," he includes.

"How will they explain her coming back with a suntan?"

"Who cares?" Cole scoffs. "We'll be going with her."

"Really?"

"Really," Cole says, "so if you have a preference between Italy and France, you should let her know soon."

"I've never even left the country before."

Cole says, "What's that got to do with anything?"

"Nothing, I guess. But when is it she wants to go?"

"She films her final scenes in the next couple of weeks," Cole says before taking a sip of his drink.

"Peachy. But what about you," I ask him, "Italy or France?"

Cole shrugs. "I don't like the French," he admits. "I can't name a great actor or musician or artist to come from France in the last hundred or more so years, but they still have this fucking attitude. But if we go to Italy," he adds, "we'll have people pushing religion down our throats. You think that TV preacher, King, is it? Chambers knows is a dick, I'm guessing there'll be a lot worse than him over in Italy."

"So where would you prefer to go?"

"Germany," Cole grins. "Late night bars and clubs, whores, stronger beer and drugs… Germany is where I want to go. I just wanted you to set your heart on Italy or France," he jokes.

46

Despite the Prozac I swallowed, the heat has kept me from sleeping again. If I'd spent the night at Tiffany's place, I could have slept no problem. The air conditioning over at her place would have kept me cool, or I could have gone outside and slept on a sun lounger beside the pool. But I didn't spend the night at Tiffany's, I stayed here at Saint Claire's. There's been no breeze at all, so all we've had coming in through the broken windows up on the next floor is yet more heat. Heavy, suffocating air has taken over every inch of the building and I can't sleep with my door open because the heat only has me notice the smell of something rotting away thanks to the water that comes in whenever it rains if I keep my door open.

"Fuck," I say, taking the cigarettes from the nearby jeans I discarded late last night or early this morning. I'm on my gym mat, wearing nothing but my underwear. My sleeping bag, blanket and clothes are all around me. With the cigarette hanging from my lip, I pull on my jeans and slip my bare feet into my shoes before heading to the kitchen. The door to Doyle's room is standing wide open so I take a peek inside to see if he's awake but he's fast asleep. He's rolled off his gym mat during the night, pulled enough of his sleeping bag to cover one shoulder but nothing else. As always, he went to bed wearing nothing more than his underpants. His nuts are hanging clear out of them like they're on display or something.

In the kitchen, I take what I need from the refrigerator to make a cup of instant coffee and take one of the towels from a nearby cupboard. I have to shake a little mouse or rat shit from the towel but think nothing of it. The coffee tastes cheap and maybe a little stale but I drink it down, wash the cup and spoon I've used and return everything to the safety of the refrigerator before heading down into the basement to take a shower. I can hear the water running from the locker area and I *know* it's got to be Owen down here but, just in case somebody else has stumbled upon our private domain, I keep my clothes on and take a look before undressing. It is Owen, just as I'd suspected. It is Owen who is yet to notice me. It is Owen who is completely naked so all the lesions and scabs marking his body are on display for the world to see. It is Owen who is jerking-off in the shower area we all use despite the fact he has AIDS. "Jesus Christ," I hiss.

"What?" Owen says, turning in surprise to see who has caught him. Maybe it's the surprise that prevents him from releasing his boner, or at least trying to cover it. "Oh," he laughs. "This is a little awkward, isn't it?"

I don't see the humour of the current situation. I don't see anything funny about a man with AIDS casting his spunk all over the shower area we have to share. "Jesus Christ," I say, "what the fuck are you doing?"

"Well," he smirks, "what does it look like?"

"This isn't fucking funny!" I yell and I have to stop myself from marching right over to him and punching him in the nose. I stop myself from punching him because the last thing I want is to get his blood on me. "You can't do that in here," I tell him, "even I don't do that in here!"

"What's *that* supposed to mean," he asks- dropping his hands to his side as he straightens his posture, "even *you* don't do that in here?"

"What the fuck do you think it means, you dumb," I spit- staggering over my own words I'm that angry, "dumb…"

"Dumb…?"

"Dumb…"

"Say it," he challenges.

"Fuck off out of here," I tell him, turning to walk out of the basement and back to my own space.

"Say it," he calls after me. I tell him to fuck off and I carry on walking, but it's soon clear to see he's wrapped a towel around his waist and is following me back upstairs. "Go on," he shouts at me, "say it!"

"Say what?" I yell back at him, desperate to put some distance between me and him for fear of what I might do. I don't want to hit him and it's not only for fear of getting his infected blood on me but for fear of killing him, that's how weak he looks these days.

"What you were going to say," he yells, "you redneck rent-boy!"

"Have you got a problem with me?" I hiss, turning to face him despite my better judgement. He stops walking so there's a good twelve feet or so between us. "Well?" I growl, "Have you got a fucking problem with me?"

"Hey," Doyle says, rushing out from his room in his underwear. I hadn't even realised we'd made it so close to his room. "What's all this?" he asks. "What the fuck's the matter?"

"Your boy Lee," Owen shouts out before I can answer the question, "just called me *nigger*!"

"What?" I exclaim. "I didn't call you that!" I say, more than a little offended at the bullshit he's peddling.

"You were going to."

"I was not!" I yell back at him, just as loud.

"Yeah?" Owen shouts, "So what *was* you about to say?"

"Come on," Doyle says, stepping between us to try and act as peacemaker. Neither me nor Owen had taken a single step forward but now Doyle's out here, Owen is only too happy to move forward like the tough guy. Doyle claims, "There's been a misunderstanding here,"

"This prick was jerking-off in the shower," I say.

"So?" Doyle asks.

"Are you fucking serious?" I state, "Owen was jerking-off in the fucking shower! *Owen*!" I repeat for emphasis alone.

"Oh," Owen spits, "I am sorry! Should I be out in the fields, suh? Out picking cotton for you?"

"Drop the racist shit," I warn him before turning back to face Doyle. "You really have no problem with what he's doing? Think about it," I challenge him. "Do you really have no problem with what he's doing?"

"Well…" Doyle shrugs, "I don't know… Water will get rid of it anyway, right?"

"I think his problem is how the water won't rid me of my colour," Owen says from behind him.

"Doyle," I say, "I want him out of here and I want him out of here now. I'm fucking serious."

"Come on," Doyle says, "this can all be resolved."

"Doyle," I say, "I'm not fooling around here. Either this asshole goes or I'm gone."

Doyle drops his hands to his side and slowly shakes his head from side to side. "Kid," he says to me, "you've got to understand-"

"I understand," I laugh, heading to my room. "I'm packing my bag and then I'm out of here."

"Come on," Doyle says, "this is all so unnecessary!"

"Let the boy go," Owen says right as I walk into my room. "He'll be glad he can go back to wearing his nice white pyjamas with the pointed hood now I won't be able to see him in them."

47

RELIEF WASHES OVER me as Tiffany comes to the line, accepting my reverse-charge call. "Lee," she happily announces, "it's good to hear from you so soon."

"Thank God," I sigh, "I was scared you'd be working today and I wouldn't be able to get in touch with you."

"Lee," she asks with genuine concern, "what's the matter, baby? What's wrong?"

"I have nowhere to go," I tell her. "I'm on the fucking streets and with nowhere to go."

"Lee," she says, "calm down. Now," she asks, "where are you?"

"I don't know," I sigh. "A payphone. I'm not sure what street I'm on."

"Take a look," Tiffany says, "and I'll come down and pick you up right away."

I look at the nearest buildings but fail to spot anything worthwhile. "I don't know," I tell her, "I don't know the name of the place."

"Can you find your way around Los Angeles from where you are right now?"

"Sure," I say, "I guess."

"Then where should I pick you up?" Tiffany says, "I'm going to head out to pick you up as soon as you hang up."

"I don't know," I say, scratching at my chin. "I could meet you at the usual bus station?"

"I'm on it," she says. "I'll be there as quickly as I can."

I thank her, hang up and turn to leave but turn back on realising how close I was to leaving my rucksack behind. I pick it up from a floor frequently pissed on by stray dogs and hoboes alike, tossing it over my shoulder while lighting a cigarette. I wonder if Doyle knows I've left for good or if he thinks I was only bluffing. I wonder if Owen really does believe I'm a racist asshole or whether he was just pretending; to get rid of me so he could have Doyle to himself.

I realise the two of them mean shit to me now and carry on walking. A bum with no shirt or shoes on but a thick woolly hat despite the heat takes large strides towards me from a shop doorway, his body glistening with sweat. He has a tattoo of a peacock fighting a rattlesnake on the left side of his chest, long faded with age. "Hey," he asks, "have you got a couple of bucks so I can get a bus home? I have keys," he adds on reaching deep inside his pockets, "I'm not an addict or anything like that."

"Go fuck yourself," I tell him without slowing down.

"Fuck myself?" he shouts without taking another step alongside me. "Go and fuck your brother!"

"My brother is dead," I say over my shoulder.

Tiffany pulls up near the bus stop in her BMW a matter of minutes after I arrive there. I pick up my bag, walk over to the vehicle and climb into the passenger side. I only notice the green facemask she's wearing once I'm sitting next to her. "Lee," she says, trying to make out it's all a much bigger deal than it really is, "what's happened?"

"Doyle's tossed me out," I say. I already have an idea that she'll only be all too happy to have me move in with her and Cole but I figure making things sound a little worse than they really are will only make her feel better for it. Like she's committing some selfless act or something. "I don't have a place to go. Everything I own is in this fucking rucksack."

"God," she says, lighting two Millbrook cigarettes with the car's cigarette lighter before handing one over to me, "and I thought men of the cloth were supposed to be different. What was it about?" she asks.

"You mean his throwing me onto the street?" I shake my head on trying to make sense of the current situation. "He went and sided with an old friend of his," I tell her. "We almost came to blows this morning," I say, making a point of not making it clear who exactly I nearly came to blows with.

Tiffany shakes her head from side to side. "What are you going to do now?"

"I don't know," I sigh. "I know I'm asking a lot here, but could

I stay with you? Only for a while," I say, "only until I have my shit sorted."

"Lee," she smiles, "you don't even have to ask. You can stay with me for as long as you like, you should know that by now."

"I don't want to be a burden."

"Lee," she says without dropping the smile, "I can't think of anything better than us all being under the one roof."

"Well," I say with a smile of my own, "if you're sure it's no bother..."

"It's no bother. Now," she says on holding her arms out for a hug, "come and give momma a hug." I do as she asks and she pecks me on the cheek. She laughs as we separate says, "You've got some of my facemask on your chin."

48

GUNNAR MARSDEN ARRIVES at the party some time *beyond* fashionably late. The party Tiffany has thrown in his honour. He's leaving the show having been offered two movie roles. They're relatively small movies and he isn't the lead, but it's as good a start as any. I'm standing beside the pool with Cole next to me. As usual, I'm dressed entirely in black and he's dressed entirely in white. TV folk are milling all around us, some actors and actresses, some producers, writers, directors, agents, network executives etc. They're all very good looking and will happily stand and talk with you all night as long as you keep the conversation on them. It's Cole that says, "And here's the man of the hour," to draw my attention to Gunnar, wearing a black shirt open at the collar with blue jeans and beaten Converse sneakers. It's a joke, his wearing beaten Converse sneakers. He probably has somebody to wear them for him until they look that way.

I ask, "On his own?" while lifting the glass of Jim Beam to my mouth.

"Looks that way," Cole says. "Can't be because he's queer, because everybody here knows already... Maybe he's heard some people are a little upset at his success?"

"What's that got to do with anything?"

"Get a picture of him being romantic with some guy," Cole explains, "and make sure the press get a hold of it. End Gunnar's Hollywood career before it even begins."

We watch as Tiffany makes a beeline for Gunnar, pecks him on the cheek and leads him by the hand to meet a few other people. "Well," I say, "I hope they're as excited as we are that he finally made it."

Tori Truman strolls out of the kitchen wearing a swimming costume, acting like she's a little ashamed that all eyes are now on her, and she climbs into the pool with a big grin on her face.

Tori is seventeen and plays Tiffany's long-lost daughter on the show. Tori is incredibly beautiful, so both Cole and I are only all too happy to remain beside the pool as she takes to swimming and giggling. "Isn't she something?" I ask, lighting a cigarette.

"Definitely," Cole agrees. "I heard she has quite a few movie producers desperate to have her in their next film."

"Where'd you hear that?"

"It was in a glossy magazine I flicked through at the dentist's. Jesus," Cole says appreciatively, "check out that ass. Can you imagine how happy you would be if she asked for a rim job? I'd fucking work that balloon-knot of hers like my life depended on it!"

"Says the very same man who won't eat pussy," I chuckle.

"Pussy's an acquired taste," he claims. "Once you get a bit of ass, you can't keep yourself from going back for more."

Tori kicks away from the side of the pool, taking to the backstroke. "Tits are good, too," I say.

"I'm hoping to get a shot of camel toe," Cole admits as he takes his bottle of beer to his lips. "Fuck. Do you think she's a virgin?"

"I don't know," I shrug. "Seventeen and has been appearing on television since she was fifteen or younger... Some director or producer must have finger-banged her at least."

"Lucky guy." Cole takes a deep breath. "You know who she looks like?"

"I don't know," I ask, "who?"

Cole says, "She looks like Kate Beckinsale."

I take a closer look at Tori. "You think? I don't really see it."

"Trust me," Cole says, "in a few years time she'll look just like her." He then waits a second or two before asking, "You think she takes it up the ass?"

"She's a girl of the twenty-first century," I say. "All girls from her generation are up for that."

I spot Chambers as he comes walking out of the house carrying a tall glass of red wine. He looks a little uncomfortable with there being so many people here and that surprises me. I'd have thought a party like this would be exactly what he was interested in, but it clearly isn't the case. I watch him as he looks over to Tiffany, still showing Gunnar off to a group of people and tries to decide on whether he should join them or not. I ask Cole, "What's with Chambers today?"

"Fucked if I know," Cole says with a shrug, "or care. That guy is still in my bad books."

"Yeah?" I ask, "What's he gone and done now?"

"Stupid prick called me an asshole."

"Jesus," I chuckle, "I'm always calling you that."

"You are," Cole laughs throwing an arm over my shoulder, "but you're my fucking bro! Jesus," he adds watching Tori slowly climb out of the pool, "won't you look at that? I swear," he says, "I'd turn my back on *all* of this for just a couple of pictures of her. Naked, obviously but she doesn't have to be showing her pink asshole or parting her legs real wide. I'd just like a couple of good shots of her without any clothes on that nobody else will ever see."

"You're the last of the great romantics," I joke, gently slapping him on the cheek. "But what would Samantha say if she heard that?"

Cole shrugs. "She had her chance and she blew it."

"Did she now?" I laugh.

"Yep."

"Wait a minute - are you telling me you *actually* hit on Samantha."

"You know it."

"Fuck," I say, taken aback. "When was this?"

"When we were all in France," Cole says like it's no big deal.

"Shit," I chuckle in disbelief, "I didn't know that! You hit on her in France?"

"Sure did," Cole nods. "Said she isn't interested."

"Man," I say, "I'm sorry."

"Don't be," Cole shrugs. "If she'd wanted me, we would have been living in a shitty little apartment right now with no money. She did me a real favour now that I think about it."

49

My Rolex says it's after midnight, so my nineteenth birthday has officially gone by unnoticed. I'd kind of expected Tiffany to have remembered that it was my birthday, even if she had believed me to be… twenty-four. I think. But there was no mention of it. No mention whatsoever. I can't figure out if she plain forgot or whether she doesn't like to admit I'm getting older, because she'd then have to admit that she's also getting older. I can't even figure out whether I care. I haven't needed to lie or struggle for so long now and you'd think that I'd be happy because of it but I'm not. There's no excitement or sense of adventure here. No thrill or wonder. Even Tiffany's head has long turned boring. Whenever she goes beneath the covers, I'll shudder every once in a while like I'm really getting a kick out of what she's doing but I'm not. I even look to the digital clock, wait a couple of minutes and then pull her up so she'll think I was close to filling her mouth with my nut milk. Anything to spare the feelings of a lady, am I right?

Cole appears at the patio doors and on spotting me sitting on one of the sun loungers, he lights a cigarette before coming out to join me. "Hey," he says on taking the empty sun lounger beside me, "the heat too much for you?"

"Yeah," I sigh. Cole nods as if in understanding. He saw back in France just how uncomfortable I can feel when it's a little too hot. "How about you," I ask him, "how come you're not asleep?"

"I took two lines not too long ago," he says. "I'm feeling pretty restless."

"I feel you," I say and this time it's my turn to nod in understanding.

"It's more than that," Cole says after a second or two. "I know it is."

I ask, "What do you mean?"

"I don't know," he admits. "I just have a feeling that something else is troubling you. I know you can't stand the heat," he says, "but it's not that. Not *just* that, anyway."

"It's nothing," I reassure him, lighting a cigarette. "It's like I've only just realised how fast the time goes by when you're here."

"If you're lucky," Cole says. "It drags by for me. It's probably why I'm doing more and more blow."

"No," I say without meaning to, "you're doing more and more because you have a problem."

"Tell me about it," Cole smirks. We both sit in silence for a moment, first we look at the lights of the nearby homes but then we look to the lights in the night sky. "Do you remember what I told you when we were first getting to know each other?" he asks.

"What about?"

"How it's like a prison here."

"Sure," I nod, "I remember that."

"Good," he smiles. "I bet you didn't believe me at first. It's okay," he tells me, "you don't have to lie. I know you didn't believe me back then. I could see it in your eyes."

"You mind if I ask you something?"

"Ask me anything you want," he replies.

"If you feel like that," I ask him, "why don't you leave?"

"Couple of reasons," he says. "I don't have anyplace to go," he explains, "not now, anyway. And sometimes I feel like I'm here for a reason. I'm not saying it's fate or something like that. I'm thinking I could be here as some kind of penance. I've done shit I'm not too proud of."

"This is Los Angeles," I tell him, "everybody here has."

"True," he laughs. "Anyway," he says, "you want to know what I know? Sure you do. I overheard Tiffany and Chambers. Guess what she's considering?" he asks.

"I don't know," I say. "What is she considering?"

Cole sniggers and takes a drag on his cigarette, like he's hoping it will calm him down a little. "Scientology," he grins. "The show's getting a new producer," he explains, "nicknamed 'The Axe Man' because he gets rid of a lot of people - actors, writers, everything whenever he joins a show. Chambers looked into the guy and found out he's a dedicated Scientologist and he just happens to keep his fellow Scientologists in employment. Has even helped further the careers of some."

"I don't like the idea of this."

"No," Cole says, "neither do I. You know once you're a Scientologist, you're supposed to keep away from people that aren't?"

"Sure," I nod, "I'd heard that."

"So we'd have to join," Cole says, "and they have that whole corrupt, evil business… You know, were they record you confessing the things you're most ashamed of doing, just so they can have dirt on you and use it against you if they have to? I don't want anything like that being kept over me."

"I don't think anybody does. Have you tried talking it over with Tiffany?"

"She's probably hoping they'd set her up with some hot young actor," he smirks. "I wouldn't put it past them to have some kind of… Some kind of, I don't know, breeding initiative or something."

"Making sure the next generation of successful actors and models follow Scientology."

"Exactly," Cole says. "Look at how more and more actors are going into politics. They're all Republican," he continues, "and Republicans are motivated by money and greed. You ask me, Scientologists share those same interests."

"Maybe," I say, "but this is America. To some extent, we're *all* motivated by money and greed. Look at us. Look at where we are right now and *why* we're here."

Cole laughs, getting to his feet. "And on that comedown," he says, "I'm hitting the sack. You coming?"

"In a little while," I tell him. "I'll just have a hot chocolate and a smoke."

50

Naked, I stand beneath the running showerhead with the lights off as she gives me head. Despite just how dark it is, I can see her remarkably well. I can see how she's ballooned in weight. She's twice as wide as me. I can see her frizzy, unkempt hair. I can also see her large, drooping breasts. Between finger and thumb, her hard nipples remind me of dried hotdog ends.

The head feels good but I'm wanting it to end already so I pull myself free and jack-off onto her tongue. She swallows, wipes her mouth across the back of her hand and walks out of the room muttering something about not wanting her partner to know. I step out of the shower, just to turn on the lights, and then I'm back under the showerhead. I stay in the shower because I'm convinced that doing this will stop her old man from being suspicious about what exactly is going on under his roof. Once I'm finished, I wrap a white cotton towel around my waist and head out of the room. Her other half is waiting for me. He grabs me by the throat and holds a small blade beneath my eyes. "How," Uncle Nick asks me, "could you treat your mother like that?"

I wake and spend a moment trying to figure out what the dream meant but I spend even longer trying to convince myself how I never dreamt it to begin with. Tiffany is fast asleep with her breasts exposed. Silicone implants that are starting to move and will have to be replaced pretty soon. Cole is beside her, on his front and fast asleep with left arm beneath his chin. It's Cole I'll miss the most.

I silently get out of the bed and change into my clothes. There's just enough early morning light for me to see what I'm doing. Dressed, I creep into the walk-in wardrobe and pull my old rucksack out from beneath one of the shelves. The rucksack is still dirty and pulling it free only brings its awful smell to my attention.

I never allowed Tiffany or any of the maids to clean it. Not once.

I toss a couple of black shirts and a couple of black jeans into the bag, zip it up and walk back into the bedroom. Tiffany and Cole are still asleep. They haven't moved an inch. I consider waking Cole but decide against it. Instead I quietly walk out of the room and down the stairs. I deactivate the alarm at the front door, step outside and turn the alarm back on before closing the door behind me for the final time. The BMW is unlocked, just as I knew it would be. Even if I could drive, I wouldn't take it. It wouldn't be of any real use to me. All I do is take the security card from the glove compartment before gently closing the door and walk on without looking back once.

After a while, I reach the manned perimeter. A sneering guard steps out of his little booth with his fingertips already touching the can of pepper spray holstered at his hip. "Can I help you?" he asks. I take the card from my pocket and show it to him. You see the disappointment in his eyes, like he was sure today would be the day he would get to hurt a trespasser or just some unfortunate son of a bitch who left his card back at the house. "Good morning," he says on raising the barrier for me, "sir."

I don't thank him. I don't say a single thing until I've taken my very first step out to freedom and then I stop, slowly turning to face him. "Here," I say on holding the card out for him to take. "Make sure Miss Lily gets this back, would you?"

"Is she picking you up?" he asks taking the card from me.

I tell him, "No."

He looks to the card and then back at me, struggling to make sense of what is going on here. He's been in such a cushy job for so long he's allowed most of his brain cells to go and quit on him. "You can't come back in here without this," he says on holding the card up.

"I'm not coming back," I say, and then I take to walking again as I light my first cigarette of the morning. The air is cool but I'm sure it's going to get a lot hotter as the day progresses.

51

I sit in a twenty-four-hour cafe with a small cup of black coffee and a newspaper somebody has already managed to leave behind. There's only one middle-aged woman at work and only one other customer, a long distance trucker or something who keeps his head bowed so he can look for the answer to something important in the dark reflection of his coffee. I read next to every article in the newspaper but they're all meaningless. The only one that comes even close to interesting me is on a chat-show host called Randall Berman and that's because Tiffany introduced me to him and his much younger girlfriend, a pornstar, at a party once. But I carry on reading the printed words until the sports' section begins and I take that as my cue to close the newspaper and drain my cup of coffee before getting to my feet and leaving.

I light another cigarette the moment I'm outside and carry on walking. I know I'll have smoked a good few more before I reach where it is I'm headed.

52

Saint Claire's stands as a ruined temple. The colour itself looks to have bled from the bricks of the building. Corrugated iron now covers the first floor windows and the strong material is covered in gang tags and, in a number of places, burn marks. What I find most confusing about the boarded windows of the first floor is the fact there is no longer a front door. Anybody can come and go as they please. And there's something else… Something different I can't quite put my finger on, but if this place was an eyesore last time I was here, you're about to lose the eye.

I take my first steps into the building. The stench is overpowering. It's a smell of piss, shit, mould and degradation. The tiles on the floor are caked in dirt. The lockers have been utterly demolished in a random act of destruction, as have large patches of wall where somebody has taken a sledgehammer for no other reason than to cause damage. I have to step over a soiled condom just to reach my former room. I take a deep breath, push the door open and step inside. It's hard not to cry, seeing how all the desks and chairs have been smashed and piled high before finally being set alight. Even the blackened remains of my sleeping bag and old gym mat can be seen. The ceiling is black with soot. It's a wonder the entire building wasn't cast ablaze. Spray-painted across an entire wall is the message SINDI IS HOT.

I light a cigarette and lean against the nearest wall struggling to take in such mindless behaviour, but the real reason for my remaining here is the fear I'm currently feeling. I'm scared that I'll walk into Doyle's room and find him to be gone or worse.

I finish my cigarette, drop it to my feet and step on it before making my way to Doyle's room on unsteady legs. My heart jumps to the back of my throat as I near the door and - looking through the glass panel, see him sleeping on his gym mat. Fully clothed, he's dressed as he always was. His clothes still black, his dog collar still only off-white after all this time. I ease the door open and step into his sanctuary, take delight in watching how his chest is rising and falling. I take another step forward and almost jump out of my skin as he suddenly sits, wide awake, with a look of confusion in his eyes and a knife in his right hand. "Jesus!" I yell and for a moment, we remain motionless.

"Lee," he finally says with a smile, lowering the weapon he holds so he can take his cigarettes and lighter from his breast pocket. "The prodigal son has returned," he says lighting up.

I ask him, "How're you doing?" and notice the split lip he has as I'm doing it.

"I'm a little tired," he replies whilst stretching. "You?"

"The same," I say with a smile.

"Man," he says on looking me over, "those are real fine clothes you're sporting. Somebody sure has his shit in order."

"I wish," I smirk. I give him a while to say something but he doesn't, so I continue making the conversation for us. "Where's Owen?" I ask.

"Dead," he says. "Took an overdose in a nearby park not long after you upped and went."

"I'm sorry to hear that."

"Don't be," Doyle says. "Despite his talk of dying comfortably in a hospital bed, he was scared. I can understand him being scared," he adds, "and I can understand how that could make him act the asshole."

I wonder if that's Doyle's way of saying he always knew I wasn't some racist from a small town but I don't ask him to confirm it one way or the other. "What happened here?"

"Drug pushers found out about the science labs being in working order," he says. "That had shit happen with their competitors and then the cops finally got involved. I thought it'd never end," he sighs. "But it did… eventually. City finally turned off the gas supply to stop others from trying to take it over. The building still gets water but no electricity or gas."

"Remember how you told me you had an idea *why* the place was still getting all of that?" I ask him.

"Yeah," he nods, rubbing at his eyes as he slowly gets to his feet. "I remember."

"Are you willing to tell me what it is?"

"It was just big business," he says. "Energy suppliers carried on charging the city for what they were sending here and in return, they'd be slipping the city council some of the money. But that's all done with."

"Why didn't you move someplace else?"

"I don't know anywhere else," he tells me. "Anyway, follow me and I'll show you what's changed."

He leads me into one of the nearby rooms, where the ceiling has collapsed and you can see up into the room above. I look at the small hill of rubble and plaster and say, "When did this happen?"

"Almost a year back," he says on approaching the mound. "I think the leaking roof was responsible for it. But anyway," he adds kneeling down beside it, "you see this fungus or whatever that's on some of this?"

"Sure," I nod, "I can see it."

"Hallucinogenic," Doyle smiles back at me. "You lick enough of that and you're tripping your balls."

"Every cloud," I say with a smile of my own.

"Exactly," he says. "Come on, I'll show you the kitchen."

The refrigerator has disappeared. "Tossed out back," Doyle explains. "Workmen came, went at it with hammers and then tossed it. Same with the cupboards," he says.

The decaying corpses of rats are on the floor, still stuck to the adhesive traps that caught them. "That was the one good thing about the dealers," he explains. "Those boys sure hated rats."

I light two cigarettes and hand one over to him. It takes him a second or so longer than it used to but he accepts it. "Doyle," I say, "I'm going to come straight out and say it… I want to move back in here."

"Sure," he says on taking a drag on his smoke. "I don't see why that should be a problem."

53

DOYLE GIVES A sermon on a street corner, a sermon on how it's wrong of politicians to be saying how Jesus guides them before they do the kind of shit out in the Middle East that only an Old Testament kind of God could possibly agree with, and then we gather up the money that has been dropped at his feet and walk away. I'm counting the money while Doyle rests his vocal chords, knocks back a little bottled water and lights a cigarette. "How'd we do?" he wants to know.

"Not too bad," I say, "but not too good for the time we spent out here. I'm guessing we made around ten dollars."

"Ten dollars is good enough for me. We'll head to a grocery store nearby," Doyle says, "and I'll lift while you keep them distracted. It's an easy enough job," he claims, "I was taking care of the place all on my own while you were out in Hollywood."

"Uh-huh," I say, still feeling a tad uneasy whenever he brings up my time away.

"You know," he says after a while, "you still have a bag filled with really expensive clothes, and it's not like you need all of them. I reckon we could sell a couple of things if we really had to."

"Sure," I agree, pushing the day's nine dollars and sixty-five cents into my back pocket.

"You bring any jewellery back with you?" he asks.

"No," I reply, lighting a cigarette. "I don't like jewellery. I think it's something only women should wear, unless you get married or something."

Doyle asks me, "You know what got men wearing wedding bands?"

"No," I reply, thinking he's just handed me the opening for a joke. "What got men wearing wedding bands?"

Doyle says, "The war."

"The war?" I think about it for a moment. "I don't get it."

"First World War," Doyle explains, "men took to wearing them to remind them of home. It just carried on from there. What's so funny?" he asks as soon as I start chuckling to myself.

"Nothing," I tell him, "I thought you were setting up a joke when you mentioned men wearing rings."

"Jesus," he laughs, "you've had it easy too long. You think life is all fun and games," he says, dropping the end of his cigarette in a trashcan before immediately lighting another. He drinks a little more bottled water and says, "It's too hot."

"It always is out here," I tell him. "It's either too hot or too cold."

"Yeah," Doyle says, "what was it like back at home? In Sinclair, I mean."

"I don't know," I sigh. "Dull, I guess. It was always dull."

Doyle nods as if in understanding. "Do you ever think of going back there?" he asks.

"Nah," I say with a shake of my head. "Why, do you ever think of going back home?"

"This is home."

"Amen to that," I smirk.

He leads the way into a grocery store. The only place where the heat isn't too much is right by the chilling cabinets but we have no reason to stand by them for too long. I notice a slight drop in the temperature when we're near the fruit and vegetables, like the fruit and vegetables absorb all the extra heat around them, but I'm not one hundred percent sure whether I'm just imagining it or if there's a small fan overhead. "Look at this," Doyle smirks as he picks up a music magazine with Pete Townshend and Roger Daltry on the front cover. "Magazine says there's an interview with The Who inside."

"There is," I tell him.

"No," he says, "There isn't. The third and fourth coolest members of The Who *do not* count as The Who. The Who are long gone," he says as he takes to flicking through the magazine.

"You a fan?"

"Of The Who? Not really," he says. "One or two songs but that's all. Are you?"

"Never heard a full record of theirs," I tell him, "probably nothing more than that My Generation song."

"It's not even their best one," he says before laughing. "Look who it is," he says, holding the magazine out for me to see the double page-spread on Tony Warr. "I can't believe he's still going," he sighs, turning the page again and again but Tony Warr refuses to leave us.

"Maybe he'll last," I say.

"Yeah," Doyle grins, "maybe he will. Maybe in two or more decades, he'll be in a terrible show like Ozzy Osbourne did a few years back with his whorish family. Tony Warr's fans are probably looking at him now, idolising him and thinking he only speaks the truth and is all about the music, but he'll change. Someplace down the line, they all change. Well," he says, "apart from Lemmy. Lemmy and Alice Cooper. Ha," he laughs, turning the page yet again, "speak of the Devil…"

I take a look over his shoulder expecting to see Lemmy or Alice Cooper, but it's Ozzy Osbourne standing with his mouth wide open to give you the impression he's yelling or something.

"I wonder how much he insisted they pay him for that shot?" Doyle smirks. "You know what I once read? I read his wife has sent faeces in the post to people she doesn't get on with. Seriously," he says, "a box of her own faeces."

"Is that true?"

"I don't know," he asks, "but I'd rather she sent me a box of faeces than a box containing one of her literary offerings."

54

DOYLE TAKES ONE last drag on his cigarette and then he drops it at his side as he walks on to the Liefeld and Sons family drugstore. Standing at the bus stop right across the street, I enjoy the cigarette of my own as I watch Doyle disappear inside. "Just like old times," I mutter to myself. And it really is, or it's at least a desperate attempt at trying to relive them. We ventured onto this neighbourhood purely by chance. Realising where we had found ourselves to be, Doyle couldn't resist going on in for one last score.

I drop my own cigarette in the middle of the street as I'm heading over to the store. The bell sounds as I push the door open. Liefeld looks up from his place behind the counter, open book in front of him and a pen in his hand, and nods once in my direction before looking back down at the notes he must be making. And I'm taken aback by it all, I really am. I wonder if it's the nice clothes I'm wearing that has made such a noticeable difference in the way he looks at me or if he's just really mellowed out during the last year or so, but I figure I'll never know either way.

Doyle doesn't even glance at me as I pass him; he just carries on pretending to browse. Finding myself that little bit desperate to capture old man Liefeld's attention, I take a mixture of quick-then-slow-then-quick again steps just to make a little noise. Then I turn from one aisle and onto another, ducking down low. I listen up, waiting for the sound of the door that leads back behind the counter, but hear nothing. "Fuck," I mutter and I finally notice what it is I'm kneeling down in front of. Haemorrhoid creams and specially formulated antiseptic wipes.

"Hey!" I hear a younger, stronger-sounding voice call out. "Hey!" I hear again and I breathe a sigh of relief, thinking my desperate ploy to steal a little attention has worked - until I hear the same voice add, "You get back here!"

"What is this?" Doyle calls out.

My blood freezes.

"Can't you see I am a man of God?"

I stand up as quickly as I can. The old man, Liefeld, is still positioned behind the counter but he's looking real confused. Doyle is standing *right* by the exit but another man, a guy somewhere between twenty and thirty, is pinning Doyle up against the glass. The man is wearing an apron, so I figure he's one of Liefeld's sons. "Sure you are," the man in the apron sneers, dropping one hand down to explore the pockets of Doyle's leather jacket. "Let's just see if there's anything here that shouldn't be," he says.

And then all I can hear is my own breathing and everything happening around me takes to happening *real* slow. Liefeld is already making his way over to the telephone, clearly planning on dialling 911. Doyle is still pressed against the glass and he's shouting at the younger guy but he's not trying to push him away or anything. I wonder if he's accepting that he's been caught, but then I remember what he had said to Owen, about how he'd go and kill himself if he was ever arrested again.

And then I remember how I let Doyle down. How I upped and left him for the first sniff I had of living the easy life…

I start running towards the door. I run so fast that I knock a display over and Liefeld looks up to see what's going on, which is all a part of my plan. I grab as much as I can, carry on rushing towards the door with it all in my arms. The young man turns and looks to me with confusion. "What the-" he begins, his eyes dropping from my face to the goods I'm about to rush out of the door with. In the excitement of it all, he actually pushes Doyle to one side and turns his attention on me. "You can't-" he says but I don't let him finish. I drop everything I've been running with, jumping into the air. The man looks at me in complete shock as I fly towards him with a look on my face I'm guessing is *really* crazy.

I crash right into his body and follow him as he stumbles back into a display. All the air he was holding in his lungs is knocked clean out of him a split-second before I punch him square in the jaw. Lucky for him, I was far too close to deliver a knock out blow. Turning my head to Doyle, I give him a look… A look that makes it easy to see now is his time to get out of here. The poor guy looks at me like he's unsure to whether he should take it or not.

"Son of a bitch!" the man in the apron yells out, pushing his hands underneath my armpits so he can lift me into the air. He charges me right into a shelving unit. The shelves and all the shit they were holding drop to the ground and then I drop on top of them with the man in the apron finally on top of me because of how I've wrapped my legs around his sides. I throw a left into his ribs before biting his shoulder as hard as I can. He screams out in agony and takes to twisting my ear but despite the pain it causes me, I refuse to loosen my jaws.

"Dad!" The man in the apron yells, "Dad! He's biting me! He's biting me!"

Maybe the adrenaline rush has given me super-hearing for a while but despite the noise he's making, I don't only hear the door that leads behind the counter open but I hear the bell sound as Doyle makes his way back out and onto the street.

I can taste blood and I know it isn't my own. Liefeld just about makes it into my line of vision and takes to hitting me with a broom handle, trying to pry me away from Junior. I know the cops will already be on their way but I'm sure Doyle will be long gone by then. Doyle will be gone and whatever comes next will all be worthwhile because of it.

To be continued in
"Days of Submission"

www.ingramcontent.com/pod-product-compliance
Lightning Source LLC
Chambersburg PA
CBHW050535190726
48284CB00003B/1076